# THE BROKEN NECKLACE

**Margaret Rogers**

Compugraphic Design Publishing

First published in Great Britain in 2013
by Compugraphic Design Publishing

Copyright © Margaret Rogers 2013

The right of Margaret Rogers to be identified as the author of this work has been asserted by her in accordance with the Copyright, Designs and Patent Act 1988

All rights reserved. No part of this publication may be reproduced, stored in a retrieval system, or transmitted by any means, without the prior permission in writing of the author.

ISBN 978-0-9566367-1-3

This book is sold subject to the condition that it shall not, by way of trade or otherwise, be lent, re-sold, hired out, or otherwise circulated without the publisher's prior consent in any form of binding or cover other than that in which it is published and without a similar condition including this condition being imposed on the subsequent purchaser.

Cover design by Alan Rogers

## About the Author

Margaret Rogers was born in Southampton in 1919 and lived through the Blitz while working at Marks & Spencer's store, until her home was bombed, when she and her parents took their few remaining belongings and caught a bus to the New Forest town of Fordingbridge. Within a couple of years she married local farmer Andrew.

Margaret has loved writing all her life and has had a number of letters and short articles published over the years in various magazines, her first being in the Farmers Weekly during the 1950's. Her first full-length novel, entitled "The Silent Army" and published in 2010, drew on her own experiences during the Southampton Blitz and on her husband's activities within the Auxiliary Unit, Churchill's 'Secret Army'.

She still lives in Fordingbridge and celebrated her 90th birthday in 2009.

# Acknowledgements

I should like to thank my son Alan and his wife Julie for their help over the past eighteen months that the book has been in the making; Alan read and corrected my initial drafts and then suggested improvements and alterations before arranging final publication; without his encouragement and assistance the book would never have made it into print.

I would also like to thank Martin Cooper of Marlinzo Services who formatted the final draft ready for printing.

# PROLOGUE

The necklace was only a piece of cheap costume jewellery. Certainly not pure gold, he thought. As if that Pilot Officer husband of hers could afford real gold. Unlike him. She might have taunted him for being 'unfit for military service' but he had money, plenty of it and she'd enjoyed the high life with him while her old man was away. He'd bought her expensive stuff but she'd still worn that cheap necklace her husband had given his first wife; that's what had started the fight, that and the taunting about him not being a 'real man'. "Well, I showed her," he said aloud to himself. "Silly bitch! Her husband won't be giving her any more necklaces, even supposing he's still alive."

Cheap rubbish! It had broken as he had pulled the necklace tightly round her pretty neck. The two pieces had dropped somewhere, probably on the floor and he knew he'd have to come back and try to find them once he'd got that interfering girl out of the way. He half wondered if she'd picked it up when she had suddenly come into the bedroom. He'd shouted, "Get out!" before she had chance to try to speak to Clare. Now he'd have to move fast before she started interfering, poking her nose in, asking awkward questions. Sneaky little thing, too clever by half but could be useful to him. Very, very useful. A regular little goldmine!

# ONE

# Watchampton 1940

The small market town nestled in the folds of beautiful English countryside. Neighbouring farms and small holdings brought their trade to the weekly cattle market on the west side of the town, where a row of shops, both old and new, wound their way up the centre of the high street, some of which had been trading in the same ware for many generations. A small hospital, hidden by a belt of trees, stood on the higher ground on the other side of the town.

Fate had been kind and the town had only suffered one or two attacks from enemy aircraft, and those had been during the daytime. However, the people were now becoming more frightened by the building of a small factory making the spare parts for the Spitfire aircraft, whose main factory was in the town of Southampton. People on the whole were now using their Anderson shelters built at the bottom of their garden whenever the siren went.

On the 26th of November it no longer became a choice and people made for the shelters as the warning siren shared its nerve racking sound with that of the enemy bombers' dreaded noise, always sounding worse at night. It was eleven thirty and only a few minutes before the warning sounded, an ARP warden had just arrived on the streets to start his night duty. He had looked up at the night sky and had been overcome by its beauty. Up above him was a huge curtain of dark blue silk, with thousands of bright stars sprinkled across it. It was lovely, thousands of twinkling lights. He gave a sigh of despair: There they were looking down upon us but we didn't want them, in fact they were the worst thing that could happen, a night of a million torches, lighting the way for the enemy. Ironic!

The bombs did their work: The factory and cottages had been the target and they were a direct hit. The flames lit up the surrounding area as well as the sky. The firemen were trying to save the cottages but to no avail. Fire was mainly coming from the factory, as the contents were made up of inflammable materials. The cottages had taken the blast from the bombs and, like skeletons, stood with piles of rubble at their feet.

Ted Hatch, middle-aged chief fireman was dealing with a sore face where he had broken the rules by getting too close to the heat. He asked the air-raid warden whether he had checked the shelters.

"Yes sir. The cottages were empty. The one in the centre is a bit of a mystery, you know. It is the property of a London man. No-one ever sees him, so it stands empty most of the time."

Warden Joe Brent shook his head at Ted. "You're wrong this time. One of the folk in the shelter told me there was a lighted candle for a short time on the table tonight, but there was not a sound to be heard, nor a shadow. Strange!"

"If anyone was in there, then they got up and went," muttered Ted.

The factory fire burned out at last. It was two am before the flames were under control. Small explosions from the interior were the result of the many chemicals and sprays used on the aircraft parts. It had made the task for the fireman both difficult and dangerous. The night shift had not shown up which was a life-saver. The eight skilled men from outside the town were unfortunately involved in a road accident. Their work bus had been hit by an army lorry. Fortunately, there were no serious injuries but fate had surely saved them from certain death in the factory. The ARP warden Joe did a check-up on the people in the shelters, hoping that they had not stayed in their cottages, which had been totally destroyed. With his heart racing, he looked in all of the Anderson shelters and was relieved to find that all the residents were safe. He was also aware of the empty cottage in the centre, number three. The owner of the property was a London man and only used it in the summer months. No one knew him, he kept to himself and didn't want to be seen.

It was strange: Another one of the residents said that she had seen a lighted candle in the kitchen of number three. No shadows. No sound. Her husband had wanted to knock on the door and tell the person that the warning siren was on. His frightened wife had pulled him away as incendiary bombs were already falling from the fast-approaching enemy planes. As they had hurried down the garden to the shelter, Joe listened but made no comment. Maybe the person had gone and left the candle burning. No one ever saw them.

At last the fires were under control and Chief fireman Ted Hatch took off his helmet to wipe the perspiration off his face. The Red Cross ladies had parked nearby, bringing a flask of tea. Ted was very tense. He was listening for any sounds coming from the ground beneath his feet. The chance that someone could be buried alive under all the rubble was always there.

Suddenly there was a tremor in the patch of ground a few feet away. He saw it move! He called Joe and the two men looked at the moving ground. What happened next was so strange and eerie that they were speechless with fear: A huge pile of rubble moved gently away to reveal a hole in the ground from which a child rose out like a cork out of a bottle. Stiff and more like a stone statue, she rose up and up until she appeared to hang in the air above the black hole.

Ted grabbed Joe by the arm as both of them shook like a leaf. They tried to speak but no sound came from their mouths. The child was nicely dressed like a model with not a hair out of place. She was about six or seven years old and she only looked straight through the men, her white face stiff and quite blank. A very pale yellow light seemed to come from the hole and lit her up. It only made the scene more eerie. The two men remained motionless, in fact they could not move. This was something that would remain in their memory for the rest of their lives.

It was then that the child hit the ground and stood on her feet. Ted lunged forwards and took her thin body in his arms before she fell back in the hole. She was alive!

"What's your name?" he asked gently, not wishing to frighten her.

"Jayne."

Ted carried her across to the Red Cross car as she needed to be checked over. Though un-marked, she might have internal injuries. All this time she remained silent, not answering their questions. Ted left her with them and watched while they drove her to the hospital. She was in good hands. One of the nurses was Iris Randall.

It had been a long hard night. Ted was feeling unwell with exhaustion, but duty still called. The tender had to be taken back to the station, where it would be cleaned and set ready for any further call out. It was mid morning before he got home to have some sleep.

Nurse Randall lived in the farmhouse a few yards away from Ted and his wife Gwen. On her way home she decided to call in and see how Ted was. The two families had been firm friends for many years. Gwen answered the door and told Iris that he was sound asleep already. Iris wasn't prepared for this so she just gave her the news as far as she could, then made her way across the small field to the old red brick house that was home.

Her grandmother Rose Randall had been very worried and glad to see her. Iris had lost her parents years ago, so Rose was her only living relative. The two women got on well together, and Iris knew her simply as Rose. Perhaps it was because her grandmother carried her age well, she certainly didn't look seventy five years of age. She ran the house as it had always been. People who knew her, liked her, as she was a pleasant woman with a bland sense of humour that could hide the strong person in times of trouble. She could hold her own.

# TWO

The night with all its horrors was now past, but life had to go on. It was another day. Four families were waiting in the Scout Hall just across the road, having been told to meet up there, as the welfare people were going to find them accommodation until they could be given permanent housing. The voluntary groups of helpers gave them food and hot drinks, ration books and bus passes. Sadly they could not take away the pain and anguish of losing all their possessions, some that could never replaced.

The day unfolded into a bitterly cold one, with a touch of frost in the air. After a while the light was good and a glimpse of weak sunlight played hide and seek at intervals, making the morning seem better. The next surprise was the sudden flow of people taking a look at the piles of rubble and the destroyed cottages. Soon there were crowds and they were asking about the little Miracle girl.

The police had roped off the area for public safety while the press were warned not to take pictures of the bombed factory. There were rumours that the child had flown out on golden wings from a hole in the ground. The air raid warden was highly amused, but he didn't think that it was the right time to tell anyone that there were three witnesses to the real incident of the Miracle and he was one of them. In the end, the police had to tell people that the little girl had been taken to hospital for a check up. It seemed to satisfy the crowds, but as the police sergeant remarked to his men, he hoped they wouldn't go trailing up to the hospital.

Nurse Randall had a shock when she arrived at the hospital on duty at two o clock. The amount of visitors was extraordinary for the children's ward, as there were only a few sick children there. Jayne was in one of the beds and had come out with flying colours. She was perfectly fit. The doctor was there by her bed and he told Iris about her condition. "Not even a scratch on her flawless skin," he said with a smile. "But she is still a mystery patient. Do you know there was not a speck of dust or dirt on her clothes! They were so clean and not even creased. It does not make sense."

The staff were highly amused when they had heard that she was an angel. The doctor raised his eyebrows. "I hear that she is a self-willed, very strong minded seven year old, who will only tell you what she wants you to know. She remains silent when asked some questions, such as her surname or address. We need it, nurse."

"Perhaps she has loss of memory."

"No. I have tested her, and I'm beginning to think Jayne has something to hide."

The nurse nodded her head. "I'll see what I can do with her. Jayne, you must give the Doctor your full name and address. It is important."

"Why?" Jayne stared darkly at her.

"They need it to find your next of kin."

"Well I have no intention of giving it to you or the doctor, or anyone else, come to think of it. You see, they won't find them, so stop asking silly questions."

Later the police stood by the entrance and checked on the visitors coming in. The press were not allowed in the ward as

Jayne needed protection and would have to keep in hiding for a while. Another group of visitors came towards Jayne's bed, this time the town councillor and by his side the children's welfare officer. The doctor was about to leave the bedside but they asked him to stay, also Nurse Randall. One of the staff found another chair and then drew the curtain round the bed.

The discussion lasted for thirty minutes and they tried to decide where to place Jayne until her parents had been found. Iris asked if she could look after her, as she had the right family home, with her grandmother Rose to be there for her while Iris was on duty at the hospital. Jayne wanted this. She seemed to have bonded with her nurse and friend, so there was consent from the councillor .

The town of Watchampton was new ground for Jayne. Strange yet exciting, she viewed it through the eyes of an adult, not a child. It was nice. In her mind she could picture her beloved father here with her and Iris. He would love it. The very thought of being well away from Uncle Sid was her dream. If only she did not have to set eyes on him ever again, but what if word got out that she had survived the bombing? Keeping her identity a secret had to be the answer. Jayne suddenly made up her mind: She would never reveal her surname or address. And there were to be no photos taken of her. Her hatred of the smooth-talking man, made her feel sick inside.

"You are looking very serious Jayne. You haven't changed your mind about living with us, have you?"

"Oh no. I'm so sorry; actually I was miles away in dream land."

"Well, here we are. This is the house; it's called Cherry Cottage and I was born here twenty three years ago. Both my parents died by the time I was four years old. My Grandmother brought me up, but she insisted I call her by her Christian name which is Rose."

"I was just four when my mother died and my father was there for me," said Jayne. "We had a great time together. He taught me everything I know, so I never went to school."

"No wonder you have such a high I.Q. You seem to know so much." Iris took her hand and they made their way up the path to the front door.

Rose was waiting on the step for them, and there was a big smile on her face. Shyly, Jayne put out her hand to shake it.

"I am very pleased to meet you," she said to the tall grey haired lady.

"I am too, and I should also like to add 'welcome' to you as well Jayne. Oh, and you may call me Auntie Rose. I do hope you are hungry Jayne. I've prepared a nice tea for us all. Cheese on toast, with a poached egg on the top."

"It does sound good," said Jayne. "I have never had that before."

"Well you are lucky, because cheese is rationed and eggs usually arrive dried in packets. Ted Hatch gave me four fresh eggs this morning. He keeps a few chickens in his backyard."

Jayne laughed as she told them about her stepmother's cooking. "I often had a boiled egg for my tea. It was either hard as a piece of coal, or not cooked, so that the jelly and raw egg burst over the top and made a mess. Then she used to smack me across the face."

When it was time for Jayne to go to bed, Rose took a warm brick from the range oven, she wrapped it in a small piece of pink blanket and handed it to her. "Tuck it down to the bottom of the bed. It is a very cold night. It will help you to get to sleep."

"I've never had one of those before, but if it is as nice as that tea, then I am beginning to like you, Auntie Rose."

"That's good dear. Goodnight. Sleep well."

It was her first night in the strange bed, but Iris lit the night light and made her as comfy as possible. The room was quite cold and long dark shadows hung about in the corners, dancing as the draught under the door made the flames from the night light flicker. Iris had found her a pretty eiderdown and she was now quite snug, as the brick was throwing out heat. She bent over to kiss her goodnight. All was well, then Iris made a grave mistake: With a quick move she wet her two fingers and pinched the wick of the light. Darkness took over. Jayne let out a loud scream and sat up in the bed terrified. "Please Auntie Iris; don't leave me in the dark, please."

Iris found the matches and relit the light again, feeling upset herself. "I am so sorry Jayne, I really am. I should have left it; After all, it's a night light. You are so grown up,

I didn't think. You're not like a seven year old. I am so proud of you."

A voice from the doorway startled them both. "What on earth is going on?" It was Rose standing there in her brown and white dressing gown, tall and thin and with her hair let down around her shoulders. It was a strange sight.

"It's all right Rose, go back to bed."

Iris lingered a while until Jayne had settled down, telling her a grown up story to ease the tension. Then later she crept back to her room and lay awake for hours listening.

At two o'clock in the morning, Iris went softly back to check on Jayne. She was asleep, but lashing out at the bedclothes, twisting and turning. Iris placed the blankets over her and gently held her down, but she didn't wake and after a while she quietened down, so Iris left her. As she climbed into her own bed, she began to wonder just what the seven year old had suffered whatever life had thrown at her. Was this stepmother to blame? She had difficulty getting back to sleep again for thinking about it and the others. The decision had been made for Nurse Randall to foster Jayne for a short time, until her parents were found.

Matron gave her a few days leave to get the child settled in her home, and the required paperwork, forms to be signed. There was quite a lot to do, as Iris had to talk it over with her grandmother. However, she was sure that Rose would agree. Iris had lived with her since she was born. Poor old Rose Randall had lost not only her daughter in law, but her son, so she had been forced to bring up their baby on her own.

Iris had been a very contented child and a great joy in her life but that was twenty three years ago and now it was all about to start again. Rose was excited.

Iris overslept. She looked at her bedside clock and it was eight fifteen. One thing in her favour, she didn't have to go to work. Matron had given her three days off. She washed and dressed before going in to wake Jayne up. She noticed it was very quiet as she opened the bedroom door. What faced her was the mess and disorder in the room. The bed was empty and all the bedding was scattered around on the floor. The large double wardrobe was open and Jayne was curled up in the bottom, still asleep. The light from the last of the night light was flickering on her slim body. It was certainly cosy, as she was lying on Rose's old fur coat. There were a lot of empty coat hangers on the rail. Iris could hardly believe her eyes.

"Time to get up Jayne," she said softly.

The child woke up and reached for her clothes. "I am so sorry Auntie Iris. I will put the room tidy again and remake my bed. It's all so strange, I don't know what happened. Uncle Sid was over in that corner, so I came over here where he couldn't find me, or else he would have got in my bed."

"But Jayne, we know he was not there. It was only a dream." Iris bent down and cuddled her close. They stayed for a while until Iris could feel her trembling body stop and relax. Then she helped her to the bathroom where she actually let Iris help wash and dress her.

"Auntie Rose is up already, making some lovely porridge. We'll go down and help her, shall we?"

Jayne reached out to take her hand. "You won't let her see the untidy bedroom, will you?" Iris squeezed her hand. "No of course not, that will be our little secret."

As they came down the stairs together, Iris was made more aware of the responsibility she had undertaken with this small child. She came to realize that Jayne needed some more clothes; she was now wearing her entire wardrobe. Her hair was so beautiful, but it needed attention. Iris came to terms with the needs before her and decided to do something about it; as yet another task had to be to get her to the doctor for a check up. These nightmares were not natural. They would affect her health if left to continue. Jayne needed a lot of love and tender care.

The kitchen was warm and cosy from the large old cooking stove. It burnt wood most of the time, as it was always available in the woods at the rear of the house. Jayne stood silently taking it all in, wide-eyed and excited. "This kitchen is so lovely Auntie Rose; ours at home in the flat is cold and always messy, as Clare my stepmother only ever made burnt toast for breakfast and never used the gas cooker, or cleaned it." No wonder Rose looked shocked as she asked her if she would eat porridge instead. Jayne soon set her mind at rest when she beamed with anticipation and said, "Yes!"

Later Jayne held up her empty bowl in pride as it was empty. The two women were not only pleased, but relieved. Iris had been worried that she would have lost her appetite after such a bad night. It was good to see the change in her, she seemed so happy. Before they made any more plans for the morning, Iris suggested they go upstairs and clear up

Jayne's untidy bedroom; the floor was covered in bedding and clothes from the wardrobe and, with childish enthusiasm, she enjoyed helping but was also very contrite for all the trouble she had caused. Iris turned her bed round to face the window. It changed the scenery so that she would no longer see the black dancing shadows in the corner of the room. No more nightmares. Iris also thought this time together would encourage Jayne to talk about her past in London. It would help if she could get her to say her surname, also the district in the city where her home was. Up until now she had chattered a lot, but it had been a guarded conversation and she had never let slip something she did not want you to know. In other words, she was an extremely clever child for seven years of age.

Beneath it all, Iris was quite bowled over by her fear of ever having to go back to the two people who made her life a misery with their cruelty. Her stepmother, it seemed had thought nothing of going out and not returning for several days. Strangely, Uncle Sid was often not there during that time. He was a bit of a mystery. Jayne told Iris she had to lock her bedroom door at night, as one morning she awoke to find him about to climb into her bed. However, she was taught how to defend herself by her father, so he soon gave up the idea and left. After that she obtained a key for the lock and made sure she used it every night. Her stepmother once tried to take the key away from her, but she wore it on a piece of thin strong thread around her neck.

Shocked and deep in thought, Iris wondered what would have happened if her father had arrived home on leave, but

Jayne said that he was a pilot in the Royal Air Force. He was rarely able to get leave to travel home, and then when he did he spent the time sleeping. Iris began to ask Jayne more questions. She could not understand why Jayne let Uncle Sid bring her alone to Watchampton and on her own. Why was it that the stepmother could not come with her in the car? But Jayne told her that she had been asleep and Uncle Sid didn't like to wake her up.

Jayne was lying back in the chair in the corner of the room. The story seemed to Iris to be so frail, that she didn't believe half of it. In fact, she felt a cold feeling in the pit of her stomach as she asked Jayne why he had left her in the house on her own. But Jayne's answer was even more sickening, as she said he had been going back to pick up Clare as she would have had a good sleep by then. He had left almost at once and then locked Jayne in. Iris thought that that was strange and rather cruel and she was not able to listen to Jayne's story any more.

The bedroom was nice and tidy now, so they went back downstairs to the warm kitchen. They had planned on going shopping, but there was a cash problem, so they decided to go for a little walk across the fields to the wood which was at the back of the cottage, so they went out of the back door and crossed the yard to the country landscape. Jayne was excited as being a town girl; it was all so healthy and fresh. It was also cold so they didn't stay out long. It was the first of December. It was just as well they had not gone in to the town shopping: Iris had given thought to the danger of recognition. She knew that Jayne would have to stay out of the public eye for just a little while longer, or until gossip and news had calmed down on the 'Miracle child'.

It was almost dark by the time they returned home from their walk and they were in the cosy kitchen once again, thawing out, when a knock came at the back door. Iris unbolted it and stared out in to the darkness. It was firemen Ted Hatch, who was holding a pheasant in one hand and an object wrapped in a tea-cloth in the other.

"Hello Ted, don't stand out there in the cold." Iris opened the door wide.

"Thanks, but shut the door quickly because you are breaking the law if the warden sees a light."

"It's only a candle," laughed Iris.

Ted handed her the gifts, and she unwrapped the tea-cloth to reveal a small hand-baked loaf, still warm. She hung the pheasant on the back door hook. "Thanks a lot Ted. Will you also thank Gwen for me? Rose loves a game bird; I think she said she was going over to see your wife tomorrow."

"It is thawed now and there is only mud and slush out," he said, pointing to his boots. "How is the little girl?"

"She's very happy and settled down with us. I would hate to part with her now."

"That is right," said Rose, suddenly appearing from the other room. "It's nice to see you Ted."

Iris butted in quickly, showing her the gifts he had brought for her, especially the pheasant.

"You and my Gwen go back a long way," said Ted. "I was told you were both school teachers in the old Red House."

"Shut up, it puts years on me."

"You have had a busy day Rose, with your little girl to look after."

"My goodness how quickly gossip gets around," she replied, just a little ruffled. "Have you been talking to that welfare woman? She called on me this afternoon."

"No not me, I was at work today at the station repairing my engine and hose, I think she came to our cottage in the afternoon, so Gwen said."

"What did she have to talk about?"

"I don't know. I think Gwen said she was questioning your age to be looking after a child all day. But she told the woman that your little girl is not a baby."

"For heaven's sake Ted, she has a name, Jayne, and she is seven years old now."

At the mention of her name Jayne came through into the kitchen and Rose said to him, "Ah, here she is. Jayne this is our friend Ted. Do you remember him?"

"Oh yes, would I ever forget the fireman who pulled me from the rubble? And I like you."

Ted gave her a broad smile and Jayne then shook hands with him in a very grown up way.

"Is that bird hanging on the door a pheasant and why is it there?" she asked.

"Oh I just brought it for the family's dinner. You knew what it is then?"

"Oh yes, there was always one in the window of the shop next to our house. You know, a stuffed one in a glass case."

"And where was that dear?" said Rose, hoping at last to have an address for the child; but Jayne turned away. The shutters came down. She would say no more!

Throwing caution to the wind, Ted swept her off her feet and gave her a bear hug. "You are my little angel," he said softly,

Jayne kissed him on the face, and then with a giggle, accused him of having a beard and they all laughed

They were to have one more surprise from Jayne that only added to the mystery surrounding her. "We always had turkey and game for our Christmas dinner," she said as Rose carried in the plate of roast chicken, "and the butler always twirled the dish up high on his middle finger before he placed it on the dining table." There was a moment's silence while the two women got their breath back.

"You must never tell lies," said Rose.

Jayne stiffened, her face changed from a happy laughing child to an adult full of indignation. "I do not tell lies", she said in a sharp voice. "Daddy always told me, never tell lies."

The two women were speechless. "It was a big house and we always went there for Christmas day." Jayne was reluctant to continue.

"Perhaps it was your grandfather, or an uncle," said Rose. Jayne sat in silence. Iris knew that it was no good to continue, she had discovered in the past that Jayne was strong willed. Rose broke the silence and suggested they eat the chicken or the meat would disappear with the cold, it was already shrinking. Jayne laughed and the meal continued.

The afternoon was bright, all the traces of snow had gone but there was a cold north east wind blowing across the fields. Iris had asked Jayne to accompany her to Ted Hatch's cottage, which was only across the field. Iris wanted to take their Christmas presents to them before dark. Jayne was well wrapped up, as she was wearing the thick woollen scarf that Iris and Rose had given her for Christmas.

They were just about to leave, when Iris heard someone knocking on the front door, which was at the front of the house.

"Hang on a minute." Iris ran back in quickly, as the last thing she wanted was to awaken Rose. She called out to Jayne and tried to explain the "I'm so sorry but my neighbour would like me to go to the hospital with her. She is going to visit her daughter as she is not so well today. In fact she is quite ill."

Jayne clutched hold of Iris with a pleading look on her face. "Can I come too?"

Iris looked at her friend, who nodded. "Very well, but will you just let Rose know we are going?" Iris put the bag of gifts down on the hall table, and then they closed the front door behind them and got in the grubby old van parked outside.

It only took them five minutes to reach the children's ward in the small local hospital. "Thank you Iris for coming with me, I only hope my little Molly is out of danger. She was scratched on the face by our neighbour's cat and the wound turned septic. We brought her into the hospital when she became delirious."

Iris looked at her friend in sympathy. She was older than her and had three other small children. Her husband was serving overseas with his regiment and it was difficult for her at times trying to cope on her own, growing vegetables and selling them to make a living. Iris had known her for many years.

One of the nurses came to talk to Iris as soon as they arrived. "Hello I've come with my neighbour, Kath Smith to see her daughter Molly. Yes, can you tell me what is going on?" said Iris.

"No not really." The nurse lowered her voice to a whisper. "Molly won't eat or drink and is developing a high temperature. We can't understand how a scratch like this became so badly infected. As well as the scratches she has a skin rash just around her mouth and on her neck."

"Has she been examined by the Doctor?" asked Iris.

"Yes. He forced her to open her mouth, as she refused earlier," the nurse continued. "Molly has caused a bit of worry for a little three year old. Come and have a look, Iris, only as a visitor though, as you are out of uniform."

Iris had forgotten all about Jayne, so it was a shock when she pulled aside the curtain that encircled the bed, to find Jayne, standing by the side of the bed with her mother, quietly looking down at Molly.

After a while they were asked to step outside, while the two nurses had a private discussion but Molly refused to let go of Jayne's hand. Jayne stayed as quiet as a mouse, until Kath went down the small corridor to the lady who was making cups of tea. The children's ward was filling with visitors by now and the hum of visitors' voices had reached through to the other ward.

"You really have had a busy twenty four hours," said Iris to her work mate.

"Yes, and it's worrying that she doesn't seem to be responding to the usual treatment."

They returned to the child's bedside in time to see Jayne running her hands all over Molly's face and neck.

"What on earth are you doing Jayne? Stop it." Iris spoke in the kind of voice that was always obeyed.

"Sorry Auntie Iris, but I was just making her better." Before the nurses could reply, Molly was up, sitting slightly forward and reaching to be sick. Jayne, with a swift movement, gave her a firm pat on the back. Just at that moment, Molly's mother came back. "How is she?" she asked.

"I think she's trying to be sick," replied Iris, "The nurse has gone to get a sick bowl." They looked on in amazement as Molly started to talk, asking for a drink of water. The scene that followed was so unusual that it was hard to believe. Molly stopped reaching and coughing and said, "I feel better, Mummy." It was all over so quickly; no one spoke or moved, except Jayne, this little seven year old girl who, but for her size, could be an adult.

"She'll be fine now," said Jayne.

"We must go now as the light is fading and I can't bear to go out in the blackout," said Kath.

"Yes," said Iris. "I think we had better. Don't you think your little Molly looks well? Do you know, a miracle has been at work on Molly's face. Her rash has disappeared. And so suddenly!"

As they went out of the hospital gate, the two women laughed in disbelief. Jayne looked tired and just a little emotional; the incident seemed to have drained her strength. She was quiet on the way home, even too far away in thoughts, to hear the two say their goodbyes. "Thank you for coming with me, Iris," said Kath, as she brushed her thick black hair away from her face.

Iris was on duty the following day, her hours were two until five pm. She liked the hours as they were visiting hours and the children were at their best waiting for parents. When she clocked in she noticed that little Molly, the patient in the far corner had gone home. Iris got in to conversation with the nurse who had been working with her and asked how Molly was when she left, that morning. The nurse looked in her book and said how Molly had been very poorly with a high temperature only two days before. "Do you think she was sent home too quickly after such an infection?" asked Iris.

"Well she has your foster child Jayne to thank for her cures, because she left this ward running and skipping out with her mother as healthy as a bee," said Nurse Linder. "I was telling the house doctor, that I was there and actually saw the strange unearthly miracle. It shook me so much, that I didn't have a wink of sleep last night."

23

Iris looked, and was worried, not knowing just how to explain the situation regarding Jayne. "Please don't spread this story around. The last thing she needs is publicity. Jayne is strange child, sensitive and suffering with a loss of memory on certain things in her life, making her very vulnerable to the outside world. I have to protect her; I've grown to love her in a very short time." The nurse took her hand and shook it.

"You have no need to worry on that count Iris," she said. "I'll let the whole thing rest. However, you certainly have an enormous task to have to deal with, not only now, but in the years ahead. I wouldn't like to be in your shoes!"

By the end of the week the rumours about the miracle healing had either been dismissed or disbelieved and life in the ward continued as normal. There were not a lot of children in the town, as most of them had been evacuated to safer areas. However there were four children admitted to the ward, but only one of them came under the heading, serious. Her name was Kate and she was eight years of age. Iris allowed Jayne to visit the children's ward and she became friends with Kate. In fact, all the children loved her visits, as she had a sense of humour and wit that uplifted them. In her red woolly hat and scarf she became a regular sight on the ward.

Iris had other ideas for Jayne's future, she wanted her to go to school. It had been mentioned lots of times, but Jayne would not agree. However, fate stepped in and changed her life and the life of others. Jayne suddenly announced that she needed to go to visit her friend Kate at eight thirty in the morning. Rose stared at her across the supper table. "Don't be stupid child," her voice was sharp. "They wouldn't let visitors in to the ward at that time."

Jayne went silent, but her eyes pleaded with Iris to let her have her way. It must have worked, because Iris smiled across at her and after a moment's hesitation, told her she could go in with her in the morning, but it would not be that early, as her hours were ten until two, for the next few days. Rose made a noise of disapproval but Iris winked her eye at the smiling Jayne.

When they all climbed the stairs to bed, Iris went in to Jayne's bedroom and sat on her bed. Jayne knew she wanted to talk to her. "Why do you need to go to the hospital so early in the morning?" she asked.

"No reason," said Jayne.

"Now, come on Jayne you must have some reason for all this. Is there something you are keeping from me?"

"No it is just personal, that's all."

"So much that you can't tell your best friend, me?"

"I thought the doctor did his round at eight thirty and would want to s see Kate's leg without the dressing on, then I could ask him if I could touch it. I only wanted to help. As you know, I have healing hands. Daddy knows!"

Iris was bewildered and, for the first time, she felt unable to advise this strange lovely child beside her. They sat quietly for a moment, then Iris spoke from her heart. "Now listen Jayne. You are too young to speak to a doctor on duty and with a patient too. Also, did you know Kate has a badly torn leg? It's not a nice thing to see. I have, when I dressed it."

"Did she tell you how it happened?"

"No." Jayne reached out a shaky hand and waited. Iris picked her words out carefully; it was bedtime and she softened the story. "Kate was rather naughty. She tried to get through barbed wire defences, and they are put there by the army, Jayne, for just that, to keep the enemy out. It was a silly thing to do, but I did hear from the house doctor, that Kate had been trying to rescue a little dog, which was badly injured, probably by a van or car. The tragic thing was, they had thrown the poor little thing over the roll of wire and left it, so no one could get it."

"She was very brave," said Jayne.

"So are you Jayne. You have a wonderful gift of healing with your hands, but it is too much this time for you. The time will come when you are older and this rare gift will help you in your life."

"I've already made plans to go to school with Kate. It is possible to obtain a place in her section? I am only a little younger, by about a year. I shall need more education if I'm to be a doctor."

The next moment the voice of a bad tempered Rose came up behind them. She was standing in the doorway before shuffling in to make her point. Her long dark brown dressing gown was tied round her thin frame with a thick, brown cord, making her look like a monk. "Are you going to sit here all night?" Her attitude was a mixture of self pity and fire.

As she turned to go, Jayne shouted to her, "I'm starting school soon, and with my friend Kate. That is, when she gets better."

Iris looked at her, speechless but after the shock she came back in to the room and gave Jayne a cuddle. "Oh that is good news, but we will have to wait until the morning to discuss it. We had better get some sleep now."

Jayne now in bed, looked out from the blankets and asked Iris to leave the door open. Although she had a nightlight it was a nervous streak in her as soon as the sound of aircraft arrived overhead. Iris was already aware of it, but tried to stay calm.

Very soon the shrill sound of the air raid siren filled the night. Rose was soon out of bed and shuffling along the passage toward Jayne's bedroom. She was soon in the room, sitting on the bed by the side of Iris. Then Rose made a big mistake: With a swift movement, she got up and went straight for the night-light and put it out with her two fingers. "We shouldn't have this light on," she said sharply, much to their amazement. Iris could hear Jayne crying beneath the bedclothes. The poor child was shaking with terror. Still in her dressing gown, Iris jumped in to her little bed to hold her. A rather subdued Rose had gone to find some matches to relight the night-light. Iris was furious with her. Rose, she knew was impulsive and at times a little overbearing, but she was old and had worked hard all her life. She was Rose and they loved her.

It had been a terrible night. It was not until the early hours of the morning that the nerve-racking drone of the enemy planes overhead ceased and silence replaced the horror of the night. It had been Jayne's first since the one on the day of her arrival in this small country town, since she had survived from the bombed house. Jayne had re-lived it all again in one night. The fact that she had loving caring people with her during the night was most important. It could have been much worse: Bombs had been dropped but the raid was over the neighbouring town.

Iris went to work in the morning, but she refused to take Jayne, who was in no fit state to deal with sick children. Rose was in a better mood as she prepared their breakfast. She fussed over Jayne and even said 'sorry' for closing the door as well last night. A very grown up Jayne said, "The light didn't show through those curtains. But there, you were not to know."

The old lady looked at her with raised eyebrows. "One minute you are a seven year old and the next you are a seventeen year old!" There was a wide grin on her face as she said it and Jayne could hear her chuckle as she went out to the scullery.

# THREE

When Iris got to work in the morning, she was very surprised to see the night bombers had left the town undamaged. The only bomb dropped during the night was over a mile away on the edge of the town. It had been a terrible night, as the enemy planes droned overhead and there must have been at least a hundred aircraft.

Iris found herself being asked to help on the General ward, so she paid a visit first to see Kate; it was amazing to see how much better she was, the wound was healing fast and the doctor had let her sit out for a while, to improve her circulation. It was unbelievable, some would say impossible for such a wound to heal in such a short time.

Later in the afternoon the house Doctor came once again into the ward and asked to see nurse Randall. "This is the second time we have had what is known as a miracle on this ward," he said. "Dare I ask, did your foster child Jayne touch Kate?"

"I don't think so." Iris felt uncomfortable as she spoke.

"Well the patient says she did! It appears that Jayne smoothed her leg above the bandage and also ran her little fingers over Kate's face and arms."

"I am sorry doctor that I'm unable to confirm that, but I was not there. It was visiting hours and I had left Jayne with Kate's mother, as I did have other children to attend to."

"Thank you nurse." He moved slowly away, saying, "I see you don't believe in miracles."

"No," said Iris, "I think it was the new drugs." She didn't know if he had heard her as he hurried away. It was occasions like this, which brought little stabs of fear into her, as she felt she must protect Jayne.

Later, Kate had a visitor, her mother, who looked very smart in her blue suit and tiny hat perched on the side of her head. From what Iris had heard, she came from a wealthy family and her husband was in the armed forces, a Major who unfortunately was overseas. This was a golden opportunity to discuss the subject of school with Kate's mother, Mrs. Maud Simmons.

Iris waited until the evening before telling Rose of her talk with Kate's mother about the prospective school.

"Are you going to look round and talk to the headmistress?" asked Rose. "You should, you know; perhaps it's not the kind of school that Jayne's father would approve."

"Try not to worry Rose, I'm doing my best for Jayne and you know what a fuss she made about going to a school; she dug her heels in long ago, and I couldn't move her. This sudden friendship with Kate is a chance in a million, as she actually wants to go to school now."

Iris spent the rest of the evening talking it all over with her grandmother. It was eleven o'clock before they finished and made their hot night drink. Both were very tired, but had made plans for Jayne's future education. They climbed the stairs together, but Iris could hear a faint sound coming from Jayne's bedroom, so she peeped round her door. The soft light from the flickering candle enabled her to see Jayne lying on top of the bed with most of the covers on the floor. She was talking in her sleep and Iris, who had never had children of her own, searched her brain for an answer. She didn't want to wake her. Gently she lifted her back in to bed and placed the blankets over her; still she slept, so Iris picked up the eiderdown from the floor, laying it carefully on the bed. As she was leaving the room, she heard Jayne talking softly and she managed to catch a few words, though they were slightly muddled. "Daddy, send her away from here with him.... no good... she's so cruel." Iris had tears in her eyes as she closed the bedroom door.

Sleep, when it did come was broken, her thoughts still on the child in the next bedroom. Sleep was touched with a thin thread of sadness.

The next few weeks of constant rain and a chilly east wind, made Rose grumpy and Iris over-worked with all the meetings and papers to sign at the school. However, the final news was that Jayne would start at the Penn Park School for girls for the new term, which was February the thirteenth, at nine fifteen. The uniform would not be provided, so that meant Jayne had to go shopping with Iris for a light blue blazer and a navy blue skirt, with a white cotton blouse. She was very excited, especially as Kate was now practically back to normal. Her body showed no sign of scars.

A reporter from the local newspaper had called at the hospital to take a photo of Kate, with the doctor, nurses and Jayne, but Jayne was not having any of it and fled from the ward to her secret hiding place, the hospital canteen. Iris, strong-willed but polite, refused to make any comment.

Rose bought the local paper and was relieved to see the publicity was focused on the Simmons' family. The write-up was strong, but the only remark that drew attention, was, "Seven year-old child with healing hands brings a Miracle to Watchampton Hospital!" The photos of Kate and her mother and some of the staff were quite small but clear. Iris was visible at the back of the group.

The paper was the main conversation during supper. Jayne was very quiet and ate very little. She was just about to say, "What a good job I didn't give the doctor my surname..." but stopped just in time. There was no doubt that she was quick thinking, with a brilliant brain.

Rose had been studying Jayne across the supper table. "Why weren't you in the picture?" she asked.

Jayne sat up straight before she replied, with that look of determination on her face, which they had seen all before. "I had no intention of having my photo taken," she said coolly, then she was just about to say again, "Good job I never gave doctor my surname..." but she stopped just in time. Her quick reaction made Iris realize that once Jayne's name was out, her surname would bring the dragons out of the walls.

Rose kept quiet, sensing that there was no need upsetting Jayne. What Iris didn't know, was that she had seen behind this veil of secrecy a long time ago and knew more than anyone of the terrible fear inside a very brave child.

Life however, is full of surprises. Unknown to Iris, the photographer from the other competing local paper, the 'Morning News', had waited outside. Neither Rose nor Iris generally saw the paper, so it came as a shock when their neighbor came with the paper when he brought Rose a lump of their home-made butter. It had to be another supper time discussion. Iris had worked hard to protect Jayne, but there was nothing she could do about the surprise picture in the other paper. It was fortunate for them that it was not a national daily and only the little local paper. Jayne did look a little worried, but Rose advised them to forget and push it under the carpet.

"Oh by the way, said Iris, I had to sign you on at the school, as Jayne Randall. I hope you don't mind, Jayne?"

"No of course not. I am really sorry for all the trouble I have caused you and Rose." There was a pause. "I can't remember my other name."

There followed a strange sort of silence. Rose kept her eyes down on her supper plate, but Iris looked long and hard at Jayne. When they had finished their meal, Jayne offered to help wash up. It was a nice gesture because the back scullery was very cold and dark in the evenings, with only the light from two candles. Jayne didn't like the dark, so she always watched the two candles to see they didn't go out, as they had done once before when she had been at the sink, on her own, washing up.

A few days later, when Iris was on duty, she was approached by a visitor to the ward; it was Maud Simmons. She was dressed very smartly in a tweed jacket and skirt in a beautiful chestnut colour, with a little brown felt hat on with pheasant feathers on it. She was well known, being on the hospital committee, in fact she had been chosen as lady Mayor of Watchampton a few years before. Iris knew why she had come, so went across to her. Kate, her daughter would need a good sensible companion by her side if she was to go back to school so soon. Jayne was ideal, especially health-wise, Iris could see that. However, Maud's offer to take Jayne in the family car with Kate was not what Iris wanted. Kate had made the most remarkable recovery from her injuries, enough to stir the doctors and nurses to wonder if Jayne was responsible for the speedy healing.

Now that the newspapers had got hold of the story, Iris spent a lot of her time covering it up. Mrs. Simmons found that she was not making much progress with her discussion on the school run for Kate and Jayne, so she made a move to leave, especially as Iris was busy. As she was leaving, she called out to Iris to let Jayne come and heal the little boy in the ward who was so ill, as the child's mother had apparently mentioned it to Maud. "The healer is in the national newspaper," she added. However, Iris was already at the bedside of a small child, the youngest there. If she did hear, she made no reply.

Iris felt exhausted by the time she finished her duty, in fact she was glad to arrive home and sink down in to a comfy armchair. Rose came in to her with a cup of tea. "I've got something to tell you," she said, pulling up a chair by her side and unfolding the newspaper she had in her "What about that!" She pointed to a small column of print, but it was the picture of her and the staff in the hospital that Iris stared at.

"I've already heard this news a short while ago in the ward from a visitor, hoping for the same for her son," said Iris. "It's becoming rather a worry for us."

Jayne was in her bedroom, her sanctuary, where she spent many hours either reading, or writing in her secret diary. Rose had been about to call her down for tea, but Iris however, wanted a few minutes to talk, while they were on their own. Rose was a good listener and took in all that Iris suggested. She had a plan: They must smother this healing gift that Jayne obviously had, in order to protect her in the future school years, because she feared that once the story of her gift had put its roots down in the school, it would spiral out of control and ruin her chances of education and her future. "What can we do then?" asked Rose. Iris put forward her plan of action, and they both agreed on the moves ahead: The first step would be a private talk with the headmistress and the teachers of the school which Jayne was about to enter.

Maud Simmons was at the hospital when Iris got to work. "I just called in to say Kate is fine and is looking forward to their first day of term. The bus will pick them up at nine o'clock by the war memorial. It is only ten minutes ride. Now don't forget, Monday the thirteenth of February. Oh, and see she has a lunch box with a sandwich in, as they have no canteen, except a cold drinks unit and cups of tea from the tea lady."

When Iris came home, she told the news to Rose and "We must go shopping for your uniform, Jayne."

"Where do we have to go to buy it, Auntie?"

"Here in the town, there is a big store called Millers and they have a contract with the school."

"Can we go tomorrow?"

"No, I have a long day on duty, but Wednesday I'm only on a short rota, so we will go in the morning, and get back for my two o'clock schedule."

Jayne looked happy and "Thank you, Auntie."

"I must get to work now," said Iris.

The children's ward was quiet, except for the occasional cough. There were quite a few of the younger ones with bronchitis and chest infections. One visitor called her over. "Nurse, is he going to be alright?"

Iris detected a deeper question unsaid, but she knew that tact was necessary in dealing with this anxious mother, so she replied, "Now you mustn't worry, the doctor is doing quite a lot and he is much better than when you brought him in."

She seemed satisfied, but only momentary. "Is it possible the lady healer could come in and see my son?"

Iris smiled warmly and touched her hand, then she did what she had done before, she made the usual excuses, while at the same time moving slowly "I'm afraid I have to see to another patient, so please excuse me. I am keeping an eye on him all day." It was clear that Jayne would not be able to visit the children's ward again!

Rose raised her eyebrows when all of a sudden Jayne could be heard running down the stairs. "What have you two been gossiping about down here while my back was turned?" she asked, with a wicked grin on her face. The two women looked at each other in utter amazement. It was the first time they had seen her like this.

"Is this what the thought of school does to you," said Rose. "Oh, and to answer your question, no we do not gossip, we talk. I have never seen you so happy. Are you really looking forward to school, Jayne?"

"Yes, yes I sure am. It will be a new life, and who knows, I might be able to forget that evil pair, my stepmother, and her wily boyfriend, in other words Uncle Sid."

"You'll have your friend Kate to chat to," said Rose. "Better still, you will make a lot of new friends there."

Jayne shook her head then said softly, "I only need one loyal friend. I don't like crowds. Kate is the one, but if she betrays me, I shall go it alone like I have always done." Iris followed Rose out to the scullery to pick up some cutlery, where they stood and looked at each other. "Is that child in the other room only seven years old? Makes you wonder," she muttered.

Luck was with them: It turned out a lovely bright day as Jayne and Iris got ready to go shopping. Jayne sat quietly waiting for Iris, bubbling with excitement, yet still keeping control of her emotions for a small child. It showed a remarkable amount of self discipline,

"Are you ready?" asked Rose, as she handed her a shopping basket which had seen better days.

Iris pushed it away. "I won't be needing that. You forget there's a war on and we need coupons, or have to stand in queues for hours now. Even the open market stalls are half empty." With a sudden spurt of affection, Iris took Jayne by the hand. "Come on scallywag, let's get going, and buy these school clothes."

"What is a scallywag, auntie?"

"Oh I don't know. It is just a nickname, my mummy used to call me some times, because it's fun."

"Yes, I see." Jayne pondered over it then decided it was extremely amusing. They went out and Rose waved to them from the door step, with mixed emotions.

It was only a short distance to Watchampton, so they walked it. The morning was a pleasant one, even a watery sun came out and for February that was a bonus. Quite a few people recognized Iris and greeted her warmly. She was strikingly attractive, with her slender figure, long legs and her lovely head of brown hair, with its beautiful shining copper highlights, as it hung in soft curls around her calm Grecian features. In the hospital it was all hidden under their regulation linen caps. Suddenly she felt free and so happy, with Jayne walking beside her. Deep down inside she was pretending to be a mother.

For Iris it had been her dream, just her and Richard and their little daughter. It was sad because they had planned to marry, both wanting a girl. Richard's death at Dunkirk cut her to her heart, leaving a black hole to fill with a life of nursing, lonely and cold. Then Jayne came into her empty life and days, weeks, began to change.

"Auntie, are you deep thinking?"

Iris came out of her other world; she laughed and said, "Yes I'm afraid I was, Jayne. I am sorry dear."

On entering the large shop, Mallards', Iris had been surprised to see so many people for mid-week. A few familiar faces brought a smile to her face; some had been patients on her ward in the hospital.

After browsing around the soft furnishing department, Iris came upon the children's wear. She gave a gasp of surprise when she saw who was approaching them. It was her neighbour Mrs Smith with Molly, her three year old. Jayne spotted her and went forward to take her hand. Her short stay in hospital had not left a mark and she was once again a happy active little child.

It was these thoughts that paved the conversation, only to talk of healing. The Smith family had seen the report in the local paper and she started to ask Iris a lot of questions but it was time however, to squash some of this information and with tact and kindness, Iris put an end to it, explaining how the publicity would harm a seven year old at the time of life when education needed its own space. Mrs Smith was very understanding, even agreeing to ignore any gossip on the subject.

Iris looked long and hard among the coat hangers and finally found Jayne a blazer which fitted her, plus skirt, white blouse and long socks. Jayne was so excited. Mrs Smith was still there at the counter and had bought two pairs of socks for her older boy. The two women walked together back through the footwear department, discussing the prices of shoes for school and how quickly children wear them out, scuffing along.

"I hope you know what you are letting yourself in for, sending Jayne to that school," said Mrs Smith.

"Why?" asked Iris, looking shocked and put out.

" Well, my dear, it's a high flier, very expensive. You will forever be having your hand in your purse."

"Rubbish," said Iris, "It was not mentioned when I booked her in."

"No, but the bills will arrive for the fees, you can bet that." Iris remained silent, but there was a little knot forming in her tummy. Her friend however, was keen to tell the rest of her news. "I must just warn you about Jayne's friend Kate. She is not very well liked at school; the other girls take the micky out of her."

"For goodness sake why?" Iris snapped.

"It's her mother. She has given people a reason to talk about her. Maud Simmons has a man friend, an ex-Major in the Argyle's. He has been invalided out of the War."

"So what? That's her business and I don't want to hear any more."

Iris began to show her displeasure and called Jayne who was looking at the school ties. "We have to go home now, the time is running out on us and I have to be on duty at two p.m." Iris gave a sigh of relief as she noticed that Jayne had obviously not heard the conversation.

Mrs Smith moved away saying, "I'm going to look on the shoe counter, so I will leave you Iris, but it was nice to have met up with you."

Iris and Jayne walked quickly down through the open market and suddenly decided to take a bus home, as time was the enemy. With a bit of luck there was the small local bus standing outside of the popular grocery store, Leptons', and as there was no queue they got on and took the front seat. It was only a ten minutes ride, so they were soon home.

Rose must have seen them get off the bus at the bottom of the road because she was standing on the front door-step with a wide smile on her face. Such a welcome was new to Jayne, who had never had anything like it before. In the past her stepmother had ignored her most of the time. She hung on to Rose, as she had so much to tell her and show her. Iris had never seen her so happy. The shopping trip had been a lovely morning out together, but Iris could not forget the words of scandal that her neighbour Mrs Smith had fired at her, taking Iris by surprise and dismay. It was causing doubts to linger in her mind. Was she pushing Jayne into the wrong school, solely because of Kate, her new friend? She ran up the stairs and changed her clothes for working ones. Rose had put a cup of tea on the table for her. "I haven't got time for that," she said. "See you at six o'clock."

As soon as she heard the front door shut behind Iris, Jayne clung on to Rose, following her from room to room. The poor old dear felt that she was on a whirligig: Paper bags had to be opened, clothes tried on and discussed, and of course modelled. Happy Jayne never stopped chattering.

That afternoon fireman Ted Hatch paid them a visit. He and his crew had been called out to the factory that had been bombed. The caretaker on night duty had been killed but had only just been found. Ted had been the one to discover the body which had upset him, though, mostly from the memory of that other occasion when Jayne had come up out of the rubble. The firemen had been through such a lot, and they were short of full crew, as four of them had suffered burns trying to save the factory.

The atmosphere in the kitchen changed with Ted's visit. It was quiet and sombre for a while. Rose was worn out; she drew up her armchair and sat down. Ted didn't stay long; he looked tired, just a little sad too. After he left, she closed her eyes and had a sleep.

Jayne had only the one wish and that was for her daddy so she found some writing paper and wrote him a letter. There was so much to tell him, school, clothes, and life with a foster mum who, she wrote; he just had to marry when he came home. Of course there were hundreds of things she could not tell him, but they must remain her secrets. There was just one thing however that she had to tell him; it was necessary for his own sake, so she wrote it down. "Daddy, this is important. My stepmother has let you down, and me as well. I am very happy here, so it does not matter."

When she had finished her letter she took it up to her bedroom and hid it, then as she returned to the kitchen Rose woke from her sleep and Jayne asked if she could help.

"Yes, do you know how to peel potatoes? If so you can do four of those big ones." Jayne watched her as she lifted the large brown earthenware pot from the larder containing last year's vegetable runner beans, which had been sliced and packed in layers of salt to preserve them over the winter months.

"Goodness are we having that?"

"Yes Jayne, but we have to soak them first in clean water." They worked as a team and Rose began to wonder what life would be now without this happy little girl, as she was good company. Supper was a talking point, when the meal was put on the table. Rose had made potato cakes and she had cooked the beans, but they were still salty and should have been soaked overnight. The chunks of homemade bread were accompanied by a basin of beef dripping on the table, a little of which Iris spread on Jayne's bread, using some of the golden brown jelly at the bottom of the basin.

"This is good, Auntie. Shall we save some for Daddy when he comes?"

"We'll see what we can do, won't we Rose?" said Iris. The two women looked at each other and smiled.

When Jayne had gone to bed, they had a long talk. Iris told Rose of the thing that was worrying her. "A man was following us this morning, in Mallards'. It was fairly busy for a Wednesday, but every time I looked behind me, he was there. It was queer, as he was always looking straight at us. I'm sure it was not my imagination Gran"

Rose looked serious: Iris very rarely ever called her 'Gran', only in times of stress. "You mustn't worry about this dear, it is probably one of those who has heard about the healings, and may have a sick person who has pushed him into asking you."

"What was he like?" asked Rose.

"Short, going bald, but had a good tailor, as he looked smart, but he was not young. I should say he was forty plus."

"Why wasn't he in the forces, fighting for his country?"

"You have a point there. I should have known and expected this would happen one day. Come on, let's get on to bed and just forget it for tonight. Goodnight Gran."

"Goodnight Iris."

Later when they put out their lights, they could hear the drone of enemy planes, a sound that would always be remembered for the evil throb of their different engines to our planes. There was no other sound, so they guessed that they were heading for the large towns not too far away.

Iris was the only one who was still awake at three o'clock in the morning. She was still worrying about the stalker. Her responsibility for Jayne's safety was like a brick resting on her chest; she pulled the covers down from her body and sat up in bed. How long she stayed in that position she didn't know, as sleep overtook her.

There were just four days left before Jayne started at school. Iris knew she had to make an appointment to see Mr Moore for advice. She managed to get an hour off work, to enable her to go at the visiting time which was from two o'clock until three. He welcomed Iris and on the whole it was a successful meeting. The story of the school fees was rubbish he told him, as it was a Church School. There would nothing to pay, so it was not true that she would forever be putting her hand in her pocket. Iris didn't reveal the gossip as it was private, but he had also heard rumours of Kate's home life, and he did say that if Jayne ever experienced bullying there, then to let him know.

He also stated that the uniform she had paid for would be refunded. The county would be responsible until such times when Iris would think of adoption.

Iris hurried back to the hospital and told Matron the news. "You are a brave young women nurse Randall! This is a big commitment you are taking on. Good luck in your new life; it will mean you will have to surrender your freedom as a child this age will need feeding, training in good manners, and with a gift of healing hands, she will need protecting."

# FOUR

Rose was up first, as usual, but it was also Monday morning, so she was full of action. No porridge, it was the start of the week's ration, so everyone was getting a fried rasher of bacon, one egg and a slice of bread fried in dripping.

Jayne came down and sat in her usual place. The two women watched her, wondering if she would eat it, as she was used to porridge but the answer to that worry came swiftly. "This is good, yum.. yum. Why don't we have this every day?"

Rose's face was a picture to see. "My goodness!" she said, crisply. "You, Jayne, are lucky to have this once a week. Do you know that some families make a dinner out of this bacon?"

Iris butted in. "I'm so glad you're enjoying it, it's nice to see you eat well."

"Porridge tomorrow," said Rose with a grin.

At eight o'clock there was a tap on the front door. It was Kate. "Mummy thought we should pick you up and take you to school with us." The 'us', was a tall young middle-aged man with a Scottish accent, using his car to do the journey. Kate said, "Well, it is your first day and that's why we came early, so we don't have to march in with fifty pairs of eyes staring at us."

"Good thinking," remarked Iris.

"Oh, this is Major MacTenny. He's an old friend of the family, so I have always called him Uncle Greg."

He shook hands with Iris and said with delightful smile, "Gregory MacTenny at your service."

When they reached the school, Jayne was surprised at the small classrooms and the size of the actual building, which was not as large as she expected it to be. Park Gate School was obviously an old Victorian building.

The girls started to arrive and there was a lot of noise and introductions. Jayne was not shy and found her ground. In fact the classroom became a friendly haven where Jayne felt at ease and was one of them in a very short time. The teacher was middle aged and though she was strict, she also had a great sense of humour, and laughed at the girls' jokes. With a quick move, she took Jayne to the back of the classroom and showed her a seat. "This is your place for the term now," she told her.

By the end of the day, she had got to grips with the subjects put in front of her and retained a high mark; problems only arose when there was a break in the schedule and the girls all wanted to know how she did the healing. The teacher, Miss Grey, could sense the panic in Jayne, so called the class to order. She decided that it called for a straight talk. In a few moments the order was given for no girl to mention the subject of healing again. "Jayne's foster mother," she told the class, "had made it clear that it was a very private matter. It would only bring bad publicity to the family and to the school."

By the middle of the school week Jayne felt as if she had been there for years. It was nice to spend time with girls older than her. Several of her class mates had doubted her age, and had remarked on it. "Are you sure you're only seven and not older? We've heard you have forgotten some things since the bombing."

Jayne laughed. "I'm not stupid," she said, "The only things I can't recall are my surname and where I came from. I only know it was London."

Jayne often walked home from school and Kate walked with her, but her mother often complained that it was still too dark. It was the time when people were advised to be off the roads at dusk, as there were no street lights, so the girls often took a bus ride home.

Friday was a day to remember. A cold rain had ended the school day, with the girls running for the bus and clambering aboard in the dry. It was a fairly full bus, with one or two shoppers, including a stranger at the back, who was wearing a brown felt hat and thick brown scarf. He was also wearing dark glasses.

Kate was the first to notice him and quickly turned to Jayne beside her.

"That man behind us was hanging about outside our school gates when we came out. I noticed him, as I know most of the people. There is something odd about him, as I know most of the girls' parents, and most of the dads are in the armed forces."

Jayne tried to turn and look at him, but the two girls behind them were tall and blocked her view. Five minutes later Kate had to get off the bus with four of the other girls, the two behind them and two from the front seat. Jayne felt a cold shiver and froze when the stranger moved down and sat nearer to her.

Then fate stepped in; the last girl to get on with them was sitting on her own and she hurried down and flopped in the seat with Jayne. "Do you mind?" she said. "I'm Betty Hunt."

"I know you, front seat in class." Jayne smiled at her before becoming serious. "Now listen, do you mind if I get off when you do, and if I give you a sign, will you take me in to your house, just for a few minutes?"

"Sure." Betty squeezed her arm, feeling the tension in her friend; it was obvious that she was frightened.

The bus drew up beside a row of Edwardian houses, well kept with their pure white net lace curtains. With a sudden dash, pulling Jayne with her, they got off the bus.

The two girls were stiff with fear as they stood on the narrow pavement outside Betty's home. The stranger didn't get off the bus, but way down the road was a bus stop, so the girls were prepared for his appearance.

"He's off the bus," said Betty, looking down the road.

"Can I come inside your place?" Jayne asked. Betty had the door open with her own key before there was time to reply.

It was a cosy little two bedroom house, with a nice living room, comfy chairs, and a fire set ready in the hearth.

"Sorry, my mum and dad are not home from work yet." Betty looked awkward. Jayne was standing by the window, from where she could see the stranger just outside by the gate. However, it was now dusk and she had a job to see him.

Betty locked the door and pulled the heavy curtains across. Five minutes later there was a knock on their front door. "Leave it, just keep quiet," whispered Betty. "Mum will be home first. Not long to wait, let's go in the kitchen Jayne."

They pulled the chequered cotton curtains across and Jayne spotted a figure outside the window. It was scary.

Another five minutes and Betty could hear her mother coming up the front path, but she was talking to someone and it was not the voice of her dad. Quickly Betty slid the bolt back just as her mother put her key in the door. The two girls hid behind the front door as she came in.

"No, I'm sorry but you have made a mistake. There's only my daughter here. I should try next door." She stood her ground and closed the door.

"Oh mum, am I glad to see you!" said Betty. "By the way, this is my school friend Jayne. I let her come in with us for safety, as that man outside has been following us."

"But, didn't you get the bus home?"

"Yes but he boarded the bus same time as us. We have no idea who he is. What did he have to say to you mum?"

"He asked me to tell you that he will wait and take you home. He must know you, because he said it was his daughter's friend Jayne that nurse Randall asked him to pick up from school."

"It is all lies. He is a stalker and is trying to get me to do healing, Mrs Hunt. This is the sort of thing we have had to face, all because I have the gift of healing sick people with my hands. We had a discussion only today at school over the bad publicity this has brought us."

"Oh you are the girl Jayne in the newspaper, I read about it. Never mind, stay here until my husband comes home and he'll drive you home in the van."

Betty followed her mother into the other room, telling her all the time about the strange circumstances that seemed to fall in her friend's path. She had a great respect for Jayne and they were becoming great friends. Mrs Hunt had listened with growing interest in the special gift that Jayne had in healing.

While it was rare and wonderful, it also had a dangerous side to it, as there were people out there in the world waiting to abduct Jayne in order to make money out of her skill in healing.

"Mum, can Jayne come again to our house?"

"Yes of course you can come again Jayne, you are always welcome. However, I must have a word with your dad, Betty because your little friend needs protecting."

There was a sudden click of a key in the door and in walked the man himself.

Betty's dad was a policeman, Sergeant Hunt. He was over six foot tall and with a smile that would deceive the wildest culprit.

51

Jayne looked up at him and waited in fear for the questions that she knew she would be unable to answer. Betty ran to him and he made a fuss of her; she was of course an only child.

"Who's your new friend?"

"This is my best friend Jayne," she said, but before she could say more, her mother came into the room and took over.

"John, I need to talk to you on your own. Come into the kitchen dear," she said, pulling the door shut behind them.

They were back again within five minutes. "I'm going to take you home now Jayne." He held out his hand and reassured her that she would be safe and not to be frightened. "The sooner we get you back home, the better it is for your family, as they must be wondering why you are late."

Jayne thanked Betty and her mother for having her. "Lock the door and let no one in while I'm gone," said John.

It was difficult to see the car because of the blackout. There were only small lights which were shielded on the front. He put Jayne in the front seat beside himself and they rode slowly away.

Rose and Iris were so pleased and relieved to see Jayne, though they knew nothing about the man who had been following Jayne. Sergeant John Hunt talked in private to them both for about fifteen minutes, and he suggested that he would provide a plain-close policeman to keep watch and guard Jayne as she made her way to and fro from school each day.

"Don't go out alone Jayne," he said, as he was leaving. "Always have someone with you. We have a few details of what this man looks like, though the moustache and large brown trilby hat could be a disguise. We will get him, don't worry. I am going back to the station to work on the case, casting a network of my men around the town to look out for him."

Rose walked to the front door to see him out, thanking him for all his trouble. "He'd better not lay a finger on my little angel, or he will have me to reckon with," she growled. "He's evil!"

Jayne had been listening, gaining comfort from knowing that Granny cared so much about her. With a swift gesture she ran towards her as she came back to the kitchen, wrapped her little arms around her waist and buried her face in the soft wool cardigan. It had been an emotional day for Jayne. Was the past catching up with her? It was all a bit scary.

Sleep overcame her at last that night but she had a restless one. In the morning she remembered it was a Saturday! Weekends were nice, no school, or bus, but shopping with Auntie Iris. However, when she went down to breakfast, she was surprised to see that Iris was getting ready for work.

"I am sorry Jayne. I have to go on duty this weekend, but Granny will take you out with her to do the shopping."

"Oh will she?" muttered Rose as she came in with their bowls of porridge but she smiled at Jayne and winked her eye. Iris was not so worried about leaving them as she knew they got on well together.

Time was creeping on and Rose was still reading the newspapers which were spread out on the table. "Look at this Jayne. The garage down the road was vandalized two nights ago. They stole a nice car from there. Of course it's the blackout that makes it easy for thieves. It was a nice car, a 1936 Morris tourer."

"Granny, we should be going now, look at the time!"

"Yes sorry dear, get your coat, it's chilly out. It's the first of March and a bit windy too."

They took the bus in to Watchampton but it was eleven thirty before they started shopping. Rose went first in to the butcher's and handed over her ration book.

"You haven't many coupons left Mrs Blare, but I can let you have three small lamb chops today, then that's it!"

She thanked the butcher, and then they went across to the market stall selling vegetables. She grabbed Jayne's hand. There was quite a queue waiting and Rose began talking to an old friend in front, so Jayne slipped across to the next stall, where she had seen a pretty hair clip.

Rose had bought her cabbage and was saying goodbye to her old friend, when she noticed that Jayne was no longer with her. Hurrying across to the other stall, she asked the man if he had seen where the child went.

"I dunno missus, I ain't a nursemaid! She bought a bright hair grip and that was the last I saw of her. Maybe she went off wiv her Dad."

"Did you see a man with her?"

"No, now don't keep on, I got customers to see to."

Rose felt a shiver run down her spine.

"Jayne!" she shouted, as she pushed her way through the shoppers. She was becoming hysterical now and was crying as she yelled out. "Jayne, Jayne!"

A young girl in a W.A.F. uniform, watching her with concern, hurried after Rose and grabbed her arm. "Can I help?" she said softly, putting her arm around Rose.

"Oh find her for me, please find her, she is only seven and she says someone had been following her."

The girl asked a shopkeeper for a chair and she sat her down in the shop. "My name's Margaret," said the stranger, after listening to Rose's story. "I'll go and report it at the police station, especially after what you have told me about her being followed before."

The police station was only across the road, so the girl was soon back with a young policeman. "I think you had better get her home," he said, after trying to talk to Rose who was in shock. Much to their surprise, a police car drew up at the corner of the road and out jumped sergeant Hunt.

"I've come to take you home Mrs Blare," he said, helping her up and half carrying her to the "It's best to be at home, that's where Jayne will expect you to be when we bring her home," he said. This calmed Rose, and she felt grateful for all the help she had been given. Suddenly she thought of the stranger, Margaret and realised that she had not even thanked her for her help, which made her feel bad.

When arriving home, she was surprised to see Iris waiting for her. The police had rung the hospital and Iris had been given time off to deal with the tragedy. It was now two thirty and the police had been searching for Jayne, doing their best, but were short handed, with only three constables at the station, so Hunt had phoned around other stations and passed the call, 'Child of seven missing, likely to have been kidnapped.'

Rose was still in shock. Iris was the calm one, maybe because she had to be; someone had to be in charge. The police had suggested that they stay at home, and try to stay calm, waiting for Jayne to be found. The fact that it was war time, made some moves impossible. However, the police had paid a visit to Jayne's friends, Kate, also the shops which she was likely to visit, even the large store where Iris had bought her school uniform; they all remembered her, and had agreed to keep a look out for her and the stranger who had lured her away.

# FIVE

Ted Hatch and his wife Gwen went to see Iris and Rose. Both were very upset, but their presence did help to comfort them. Iris made them all a pot of tea, but her hand shook so much, that she spilled most of it down her skirt.

After the visitors had gone and they were on their own now. Tears were running down Iris's cheek as she took the dirty cups out to the sink. When she returned, it seemed that all her body had crumpled and she staggered in to the kitchen sobbing her heart out.

Rose, her aged wrinkled face bent low, seemed hollow with pain. "Come and sit by me," she said.

Iris drew up the small chair beside her and they held hands. Rose, plagued by regret and shame, suddenly said, "Why on earth didn't we have the phone installed?"

"That would have made no difference," said Iris. "She's gone." They both wept.

The days that followed were filled with strain. There were so many things to be done, informing the school and facing up to the fact that newspaper journalists do not go away. The photos of Jayne and Iris were there staring at them on the front pages. Iris did manage to keep a photo of Rose from the press. She informed them that the old lady was ill.

Councillor Moore called on Iris who was still on leave from the Hospital. It was difficult for her, but she explained as best as she could, just how it all happened. He showed every ounce of kindness and pressed on Iris not to blame herself. In fact he paid Iris a compliment for being such a good foster parent.

It was the sixth of March and Rose's birthday. She seldom kept it up and often, had it not been for Iris, she would probably have forgotten it. On the kitchen table there was a small brown parcel in front of her when she came in with the porridge. She looked at it with a frown on her face, but didn't pick it up.

"Well, are you going to look at it? Happy birthday."

With a weak smile, she undid the parcel and finally grinned at Iris as she held out the pair of hand-knitted mittens. "Brown," she said, trying them on for size.

"Don't you like the colour?"

"Yes of course I do, I only thought how nice it would go with things. Thank you," She leaned across the table and planted a kiss on Iris's cheek.

"Do you want to go shopping granny? It's Saturday and we usually go together if I'm off work."

"Things have changed now dear. I don't feel like going now, people all staring at you. Iris, you do understand, don't you?"

"Yes of course, if you want to stay here it doesn't matter, because I won't be long. I have to go for food–bread, potatoes, meat if we have any coupons left."

"War on your insides, isn't it? There isn't much food about." They both laughed, not out of happiness, but to keep their spirits up.

Iris had only just left and there was a knock on the door. Rose went and was surprised to see Councillor Moore and Mrs Read, the Child Welfare officer.

Shaking like a leaf, she asked them in to the kitchen where there was a fire in the stove. March could be quite chilly. They sat and stared into space.

"No word about Jayne? They haven't found her yet?"

"Stupid question," said Rose, not mincing words. "She would be here, wouldn't she?"

"No," said Mrs Read, "but I think they will."

"Do you?" Rose waited for the punishment. She knew Mrs Read was dying to have a go at her over Jayne.

"You really are too old to be caring for such a small child."

'Here it comes!' thought Rose to herself, but Cllr Moore stopped Mrs Read before she could say more and said kindly, "Now don't worry Mrs Blare, none of this was your fault. I need you at the moment to sign these papers please. It is for the extra money and food coupons. We'll have to stop these until Jayne returns, which she will. I'm sure of that."

Mrs Read tried to push in and have her say, but Moore stopped her. "I think that will do for today," he said. "You will keep us informed on the case, if she comes home. I am very sad for you and nurse Randall and I hope all will be back to normal when I call next time."

As Rose closed the door on them, she felt the hot tears coming down her cheeks. She did something that she seldom did–she sat in her old armchair and gave up.

She was still there in the same armchair when Iris came home with the shopping; only now she was asleep. Iris put her food away in the cool larder, and then she too sank down in her armchair. She was so tired. It had been a painful morning, with so many people having approached her about Jayne. There had still been no sign of her. Being a nurse, Iris was well known all around the small town. She had been just coming out of Millers' shop when a stranger had approached her, wearing the blue serge uniform of the women's air force, only young, but friendly and charming. She asked if Iris was the mother of the young child that was missing. Apparently she had recognized Iris from the photo in the newspaper.

"No I am not related to Jayne," Iris had replied quickly. "I am her foster parent and had hoped to adopt her later if her real parents were never found. Why are you interested?" Iris was a little uneasily but just at that moment she could see the bus coming into the square and didn't fancy walking home with a bag of shopping so, apologising for leaving the young woman so quickly, she hurried away with a final farewell and, "See you another time."

"My name's Margaret Jones," the young woman had called after her.

Iris sat quietly thinking about the stranger until Rose woke up, glad that she had not come with her shopping. It would have upset her grandmother.

"Did you cope this morning with all the people Iris?" she asked gruffly. "I hate going off to sleep like that, especially in the daytime."

"Well, now that you are awake I will tell you who I met in the centre of the town. Someone called Margaret; she had recognized me from the photo in the newspaper."

Rose suddenly came alive, leaning forward in her chair and gasping with surprise. "I didn't expect to see her any more; I left her without even a thank you for all she did for me." Iris sat back and listened and could see Rose had a lot to tell her. "Her husband is a pilot, who was shot down during that big raid in February," Rose said, "but listen Iris, he's in a special hospital where the patients are all R A F men. The man in the next bed is in the same squadron as him. They are both badly burned and will be there for quite a while yet. Iris, are you thinking what I'm thinking?"

"No not really, it's too much of a coincidence for it to be Jayne's daddy. That was in your mind Granny?" Iris too her hand and held it for a second.

"Look dear, you must not build up hopes. We must leave it to the police to find Jayne first. I think it would be best if you pushed this 'daddy' bit out of your mind, well, for now anyway. But Margaret said that this man in the next bed is his mate, and he has a little girl by the name of Jayne."

"Yes granny, but there are hundreds of little girls with that name."

Rose shook her head in disbelief and determined to have the last word, she said to Iris, "Fate sent that stranger in to my life that day, and NOT for anything."

Iris got up. "I'm going to make us a nice cup of tea. Would you like anything with it? We never had any dinner, did we?"

"No thanks, we'll have a cooked supper. I shall do it."

Iris didn't answer, feeling that it good to let Rose have something to do but when she moved out to the back scullery to start the vegetables, she said, "No news again. They've not brought her back!"

The weekend went quickly and on Monday they had a visit from the police. Iris and Rose had just had a coffee and a cold rabbit sandwich for their lunch when there was a loud knocking at the door. It was their old friend Sgt Hunt.

"Hello Iris," he said. "They've put me in charge of this case and made me up to detective inspector. They want results before it becomes a dead end, so we're going to have to work harder and get some." He noticed Iris looking at his change of uniform and went on, "I've done plain clothes work in the past. From now on, you ask for me, no one else. Now we must sit and discuss this. There are a lot of questions I need to ask. Can I see Jayne's bedroom? Also her clothes? I need to look for tags with numbers."

Iris took him up stairs to Jayne's room where he looked closely at everything in sight.

"Oh my goodness!" said Iris. "She didn't take her piece of necklace with her; that must have upset her when she found out. Do you know inspector, that broken piece of necklace was the only thing she had with her when the firemen rescued her from the bombed house. She says that it was given to her mother by her beloved dad; always kept under her pillow."

"How did Jayne come by it? Did her step-mother die?"

"No, she told me that she had picked it up on the floor by her step-mother's chair."

"I'll take that with me," said Hunt. "It might throw some light on this case. And we might find the rest of it somewhere."

"I think you had better let granny tell you what Jayne told her about it." Iris had seen Rose hovering about in the background. It didn't take her long to fasten herself on to Hunt and relate the whole story, in fact, she told him a lot more about the unhappy years that Jayne had endured after her daddy re-married.

Detective John Hunt had been in the police force since an early age, he was a quiet man, good at his job and had a very sharp brain. His actions spoke louder than words and he never wasted them. A lot of people thought him shy but his theory was, that if you let people talk they would often let something slip out that needed to be kept secret. This job was hard and sad; anything that involved children stuck inside him on a low heat. His own daughter Betty was eight years old and he loved her with all his heart.

It had all happened so fast, it kept him awake at night thinking, just how do you find a child who has been kidnapped in a country at war? There was enormous destruction in the big cities, homeless people some still living in air raid shelters, street names and signposts had been taken down to confuse the enemy if they invaded. Hunt wondered where to start. His first move was to investigate the market, some stall holders may have seen this little girl known as Jayne, who had been with her Granny shopping in the market.

Hunt had a real problem. He worked hard spending nearly twenty four hours a day travelling around such places as seemed likely hide-outs or places where she had been seen.

Determination was touched with a little frustration plus a sharp eye, as he continued his mission to find Jayne. The police at the station were in sympathy and those who knew Jayne's foster mother tried to help by keeping their eyes sharp.

He kept in touch with Rose as she knew the town and it's people better than anyone. He also had a soft spot for Iris whom he had known for many years. She was still very upset as she had come to love Jayne deeply.

Detective inspector Hunt was also interested in the story of the hated Uncle Sid. He questioned the neighbours who had lived next door to the bombed house where Jayne was found and learned that it was owned by a stranger to Watchampton who just used it as a weekend cottage; he went by the name of Sidney Beech, never spoke to anyone much when he was there but people thought he came from London.

DI Hunt returned to Iris and Rose and was with them for over an hour. He was pleased with the afternoon's work and had learned a lot that he had not been told before.

"I think I know who it is that holds Jayne," he said to Rose as he left. He knew that he had to find the address in London of this Sid Beech but something inside kept gnawing away at him: Was Jayne still alive? Had he taken her and if so what did he want from the child? Was it the money he could make from her healing hands, or was it something to do with her stepmother? It bothered him that the child left without saying goodbye to her step-mother and, most unusual of all, to leave her asleep in a chair, with this necklace on the floor, that she had picked up so swiftly.

After having a look round at Jayne's room and possessions Inspector Hunt had formed a picture about her: For a start, the piece of necklace was a clue to her first move to Watchampton. There was something not quite right about the woman sleeping in the chair. It seemed a poor excuse for leaving her behind. Why didn't their voices wake her? Jayne didn't like her stepmother, but she said that she had left her there asleep to go off with the uncle she hated.

His first thought was to pay a visit to the council offices and seek out any paper work on his property that had been destroyed and he was extremely fortunate in his search; after much searching, the tolerant office clerk, found the rate file on Mr Sidney Beech. This also included his London address, as it had been his habit to pay the rates by cheque from Montlake SW I4. A little more searching and the clerk found the full address, which was number 9 Garton place, Montlake, London.

Thanking the elderly clerk for all his trouble, he was reminded that it was only because the police force had a right to investigate, what was otherwise private matters that he was making progress and with a smile of satisfaction, Inspector Hunt walked out to his car, muttering to himself, "I have you, uncle Sid."

That night London had another pounding from the sky.

It was impossible to make connections as communications were not possible. Once again it was like punching a brick wall, as they were no further in finding Jayne. Time too was moving on quickly, it was frustrating to all.

However, Inspector Hunt had merely rested his case, until London calmed down. The London police had been informed, there was only waiting now.

No one let that splinter of fear take over, but it haunted Rose and Iris. Was Jayne still alive? Even the police feared the worst. Rose had aged in the short time, her silver grey hair now looked dull and strands hung round her thin face. Iris tried to keep her going, but it was hard work and Rose seldom smiled these days.

Iris had got rid of the newspaper journalists. It was hard to keep seeing them around the doorstep. The pictures in the papers caused her to do some deep thinking. Did Jayne's father ever see these photos? Iris did see Margaret, the girl in the WAF uniform. They bumped into each other in the newspaper shop in the centre of town. It was a friendly meeting and as Iris was on her own, they went into a tea shop and sat talking over a cup of tea.

Margaret told Iris that her husband was making great progress; his burns had healed and it was only his broken leg that held him back. She was going to see him the next day and he should be on crutches now.

"How is the man in the next bed to him?" asked Iris. "You said his name was William and you were going to let me know his surname."

"Yes," said Margaret sadly. "His name is William Barton. Some of the pilots called him Bill, and one always named him 'Bartie.' Sadly Bill is not doing so well; he has so much on the side of his face, burns and metal pieces. These have not been removed yet. If he does make it, he will be badly disfigured for life. I wonder if he is your Jayne's father, though it is only a slim chance. Would you like me to find out a bit more about him? Mind you, I could take you with me tomorrow if you like. It's not far and I'm stationed at the balloon sight only six miles away."

Iris was staring into space, deep in thought. It was something she would like to prove. However, it was so complicated; Jayne would only add to the worry and sadness. If it was her beloved daddy, then the news of his daughter would kill him. The whole episode would have to be kept from him.

"Are you all right Iris?" Margaret touched her arm. "You look as if you've seen a ghost."

Iris shook herself. "Yes of course, that's what deep thinking does. I'm ok now. I'd like to come with you to the hospital. I have this urge to see this Bill."

It meant another cup of tea, for they talked on for a while longer, as Margaret laid out the plan for the journey. As it happened Iris had the day off, so it would mean no dispute over work.

They parted and Iris had to run for her bus home. Her heart was pounding with a mixture of fear and excitement. The fact that this Bill might end up being no relation to Jayne, didn't matter. At least she would have done her best for the little girl who had stolen her heart, then left her.

Panic overtook her when she arrived home. What was she going to tell Granny? She had a feeling that she would be set against it.

Actually Iris need not have worried, as Rose took the news in her usual way. "You are a stupid girl! It won't serve any benefit to you or the complete stranger; only confuse him more if he is not Jayne's father. But go by all means, if you must." Rose put the teapot down on the table with a bump, her face suddenly going sour. Iris took no notice, but had made up her mind to do the journey and see this pilot named Bill.

It turned out to be the most poignant of visits that Iris had ever made in her life: Walking into that hospital ward was indeed a dreadful experience. The men who had taken their young lives to protect their country, were like something out of a horror movie. Even an experienced nurse like Iris couldn't pretend to be unmoved by the sights around her.

To begin with, the staff refused to let Iris talk to Bill. Margaret tried to smooth matters, by explaining the whole situation, introducing her fiancé to Iris. He sat up in bed, one of the lucky ones who was making a fast recovery.

After a short while, the doctor came to ask Iris some questions. He was an older man and had a caring attitude towards her, seeming to understand the situation concerning Jayne. In fact, he gave Iris hope. There was another clue to the identity of this mystery Pilot Officer: The doctor said that Pilot Officer Barton had not received one word from his young wife or any news of his seven year old daughter. However, the doctor seemed more interested in the story of Jayne's life and admitted that he had never heard anything like it before in his life.

"It will need a lot of deep thought," he told Iris, "because he has to be given time to prepare for news of what could be his Jayne." He arose from the chair, lifting his hand to pull aside the surrounding. "I'm going to let you see Mr Barton," said the doctor, "but just smile if he is awake. Don't make conversation; a nurse will stand by your side."

Softly the curtains slid back to reveal what was left of a strong young man in his late thirties. One side of his face was loosely covered in bandages; the other side was red, shiny, and appeared stretched to cover his cheek bone that protruded a little. His arm and shoulder were also heavily bandaged. He slept, but there was twitching of his nerves, making sleep a sham.

Iris dragged her eyes away from the man on the bed. It was then something made her look towards the edge of the pillow, where a shiny object took her attention. It was a key ring with a tiny gold hand hanging on the circle of gold. Iris whispered to the nurse, asking what the shiny object was half under his pillow. Very gently the nurse put her fingers under the covers and brought out the token to show her.

"This is very special; he never lets it go," she said. "It's his good luck charm of course, which he carries in his pocket when on a flying mission."

"Look! It has the name 'Jayne' on the back of the tiny hand," whispered Iris.

"Yes," the nurse's face glowed with pride and admiration. "Oh yes, that is the little hand that healed. William says it worked a miracle for a five year old. Jayne is a healer, though I don't know if she still has this magic power."

Iris just stared at the nurse, unable to say a word, just stunned. In a sudden impulse she bent over the bed and tenderly kissed Bill's hand as it rested lightly on the soft white sheets. "He is the one. This is my Jayne's daddy," she told the startled nurse. "The hand proves it!"

# SIX

Iris could never remember that fateful journey home from the small military hospital. It remained a blank. Margaret Jones the W.A.F., who fate had sent to Iris in her hour of need, brought her home safely. With a story to tell among her station and a fiancé who was getting better every day, placed her on top of the world.

There had been no sightings of Jayne, even in London. DI Hunt now had more information, after obtaining an address in London for Sid Beech. While the police had no proof that he was the stalker, everyone who knew Jayne was certain that she would not have gone so readily with anyone else. The police told Iris that it was easy to trick a victim, maybe by using her daddy as a bait.

Iris didn't return to visit to Jayne's daddy: For one thing, the hospital had said that he was to have no more visitors except his close family and so far, no one had been to see or enquire about him. However, her thoughts revolved around the memory of the sick man in the hospital bed, so shattered, so vulnerable and with only a slim chance of surviving his burns and other injuries.

The girls at work were eager for news from Iris when she arrived on duty. They knew that those aircraft pilots were going through all that for them, to protect their country and stop the Germans from showering the country with bombs.

Later in the week Rose had a visit from Ted Hatch who was anxious for news of Jayne's daddy, as he had heard that Iris had found his whereabouts. Iris came home before he left and was able to give him an account of the whole visit to the hospital and the extraordinary news she had discovered while standing by Bill's bed.

"What a sheer stroke of fate!" said Ted, in surprise. "How on earth did you meet this young WAF?"

Iris told him the full story, of how poor Rose had been made ill with shock at the time of the abduction of Jayne. "Believe me Ted, she was just a stranger in the crowd, but could see how Rose was on the verge of collapse and went to help her."

"Yes, that's right," interrupted Rose, as she went out to make Ted a cup of tea. "A lovely girl called Margaret," she shouted from the back kitchen. "Is her husband getting better? He was also a pilot, shot down."

"His injuries were mostly burns on his arms and back and his face was seriously burned. He was still in a serious condition."

Margaret obtained special sick leave and paid him a visit every day, that was until he was diagnosed out of danger. However, it was only because Bill was his mate from the same squadron that made Margaret take an interest in him. The two men came down in the same fight, but had been lucky to hit firm ground, not ditch in the English Channel.

Both pilots were receiving the very best attention from both doctors and nurses. The dedication to the invalid airmen was like nothing found elsewhere. No one came to visit Bill except Margaret when she came to see her husband, who was now making good progress and was sitting out during the day.

Tension grew at home each day, the waiting for news causing frustration. Iris had her work, so had less time to dwell on matters. The ward was full with children, ranging from six to ten years of age, each having a fever which had caused a little disruption and anxiety among the staff. However, it was found to be a mild form and there were quite a lot of sighs of relief among the doctors and nurses.

Iris didn't go home for three days, but spent the nights with one of the nurses, fearing the outbreak could be infectious. Her thoughts were on Rose, who was frail these days and rather vulnerable to infections at that time. The fact that it was over in four days, was a great relief to Iris and when she returned home, Rose was in better spirits, having had Gwen Hatch staying with her at night, the pair of them quite happy with the situation.

There was also news of Sid Beech: The police had finally run him to ground back in his flat in London and had questioned him about Jayne, and about his lack of care in leaving a seven year old in a house on her own in the town of Watchampton. Sid had denied this, and swore that her stepmother had gone with her; he told the police that he had only driven them there and left them as they had seemed to be settled. Of course he had added, how was he to know there would be an air raid on the town. The questions were merely bouncing off a man who felt safe in the knowledge that Jayne was not there to verify these answers. Sid had no witnesses, so the police could not press charges.... as yet.

The Metropolitan police had to find Jayne first. They kept watch on Sid Beech's movements to see if he would eventually lead them to Jayne. Inspector Hunt made the journey up to London to work with them for a few days and his time was certainly not wasted as he was able to obtain a search warrant for the ground floor flat which had belonged to Jayne's parents. It was to prove an interesting development and a crack opened in the mystery of her disappearance. Detective Inspector Hunt was to prove a very clever man.

# SEVEN

The Inspector arrived in London, pleased to have the full cooperation of the Met in searching for the seven year old girl who went by the name Jayne Barton. He obtained a warrant to search the flat that Jayne and her parents owned in Montlake in the south west of London. The flat was one of a block in the centre of a busy street. It was not on a bus or tram route, but the street did hold a weekly market and had a few stalls set up right outside close to the pavement. Being war time, the stalls set up in their usual places, but they seemed to be less full each week. Rationing had put an end to the food stalls, and farmers no longer brought in their surplus. The most popular was the vegetable stall and of course the lady with her shows of second hand clothes.

The traders were a grand lot, providing a source of happy laughter, jokes and bright waistcoats. Also they did not resent the questioning from Inspector Hunt, but in fact they tried to help him in his search for information on Jayne, who they obviously adored. She used to come out of the flat as soon as they had set up their stalls, then would help or serve a customer, passing along to talk with everyone.

DI Hunt obtained one or two snippets of information which he stored in the back of his mind: One trader told him quietly but sharply, "Jayne's mother was so cruel to leave her on her own for days, while she went off on the razzle. Poor little child would bring her breakfast out here to eat with us, a slice of bread and jam, often no butter, none left apparently."

Hunt left them to return to the flat, his ears still ringing with promises of help in his search for Jayne. He thought deeply for a minute, because if anyone could do just that, then the traders were the ones, loyal to the grave. The flat smelt musty and strong from stale food in the bucket that stood under the sink. It had not been used for several weeks. Jayne's mother had certainly not lived here for a while.

He looked in all of the cupboards and vases for any clue as to where she may have been taken, but drew a blank; the living room was untidy with women's clothes scattered about. There was a small notebook in the sideboard drawer, and although it held no secrets, it did mention a certain friend, who was obviously being paid to carry out a simple service. What or where was a mystery. but now, at least, he had a name to go on; no surname, just the single word in small letters, 'Brian'.

He put the notebook back in the drawer and then pulled the heavy curtains back halfway as it was too dark in the room to see properly, the net curtains still providing some privacy. He stood for a moment looking out into the street where the traders were packing up their stalls to leave. As he turned away from the window, he happened to look down at the bottom of the wardrobe and noticed something shining in the light from the window. He stooped to pick it up and saw that it was it a tiny gold fastener from a necklace. It looked to be part of a longer piece of gold chain necklace and had been broken off with about a half an inch from the rest of the chain. Taking an evidence bag from his pocket, he was about to slip it inside when he reconsidered and decided to leave it where it was. He had remembered the piece of chain which Jayne had treasured so much. Was this the rest of it? If it was then someone might come looking for it and that someone might be Sid Beech.

Before he left, there was one more place he needed to look into and that Jayne's bedroom; it was the only clean and tidy room in the whole flat and Hunt went over all the little bags and purses on Jayne's dressing table. It was something he disliked doing, as he of course had an eight year old daughter himself.

He was about to call it a day, when, deep in the pocket of a little French handbag, his fingers touched on a key, too small for a door key and too large for the little jewel boxes, which he felt obliged to try out. Uncertain for a second, he then wrapped it in a piece of paper and put it in his pocket with the other items. Maybe there was a small back entrance to this flat; it was a ground floor one. Just a thought, he told himself but the key would have to wait. It opened something, but evidently that something was not in this flat.

Time was running away too fast; he knew that the station was expecting his return in the evening. He had put a lot of hours in to this case, but the feeling of frustration at not finding even a clue to where Jayne was taken made him feel that he was a loser. With a loss of pride he decided to call it a day. Locking the windows he let himself out of the flat. It was when he turned that he noticed the woman standing watching him.

With a friendly smile she asked after Jayne. "I live in the bottom flat next door. We were friends, such a lovely little girl and I thought she and her mother were back home."

"No I'm afraid not, but did you not know Jayne was missing? It has been in the newspapers."

"No I don't have a paper and I can't go out as I have an invalid husband. Jayne often came in to talk to us."

"I'm Detective Inspector Hunt," he said, shaking her by the hand. "I'm up here to try and find her. Have you any idea where she is, or where she has been taken?"

"I am sorry but I don't know; they have been gone longer than usual. It's her stepmother who goes mostly with the dentist above in the top flat but more often than not Jayne is left here on her own."

"You have known the family a long time then?" said Hunt.

"Yes, Jayne's father is a Spitfire pilot. Such a nice man; my husband liked to chat to him. He never seems to come home on leave though."

A little unsure if he had locked the flat door, Inspector Hunt put his hand in his pocket and withdrew the key again, not noticing Jayne's little key had dropped out as well and was laying at his feet.

"Inspector! You've dropped something," she said as she turned to go back in her flat.

Hunt picked up the key and made a joke about the key being useless and then, in a moment of indecision he stood on the doorstep, unsure about going in to use this key that mystified him. Something had made him stop; maybe it was these worrying thoughts about the cellar and what it might hold. It could well be that little Jayne was being held down there.

"Supposition," he said aloud to himself. He knew that, as a policeman, he must always put a cold damp sponge on his emotions. He was, nevertheless only human and he felt sick at the thought.

He walked down the path and got in his car, driving quickly back to the station where he asked to see the Super who advised him to return to the house with two of his officers and double check, using this key, in the hope that it would reveal the missing child, who could be held down there. As he said, "It may be worth looking into."

The three men opened up the flat and began their search: One of the officers had an idea and lifted a large piece of blue coloured lino up from the kitchen floor. There was a trap door beneath! He held out his hand to Hunt for the key, unlocked it, and then lifted it up to reveal a set of steps down to another door.

"I hope I can get down there, it's not very big," Hunt said. The two men looked at his size and grinned. However, needs must, so they went down one after the other, first opening the dark green door at the bottom with the same key.

The stench that hit the men as they opened up the door was evil; in fact they all put their hands over their mouths. What they had expected was a strong smell of port and sherry from the broken bottles scattered on the stone floor but this was masked by another small which came from another object on the floor: A body sat slumped against the wall; it was clearly that of a woman; one of her shoes was on her withering foot and the other one was yards away. There were marks on her neck which led Hunt to suspect that she had been strangled. The woman was fairly young but her body had been there too long for visitors. The three men left the room quickly and closed the door firmly behind them.

"One of you get back to the station and round up the forensic squad," urged Hunt. "We have to stay and keep the nosies out."

"Thank God the body was not Jayne Barton, but then, where is she? That is the question," thought Inspector Hunt. He couldn't let the words leave his mouth. That was probably Jayne's stepmother thrown against the brick wall, down there. A post mortem would give the answer to that. Where was Jayne? The question kept coming back to Hunt. If she was alive, then she was living in constant danger. He would get her too.

The Super was in one of his difficult moods. "How the hell do we get in touch with her husband?" It has been proved that this was the body of Mrs Barton, the stepmother of Jayne Barton.

"You had better get back to your station, Hunt. Will you inform her next of kin?"

"Yes sir," replied Inspector Hunt. "God, what a task, this is a sick man I have to tell. A badly damaged hero." What was even worse, he could not possibly tell him about his daughter Jayne.

"I have something to show you before you leave, come with me." The Super went to his desk and took out the coroner's preliminary report. "The coroner said she had been strangled and her body carried down to the cellar. He puts the date of death as November, that is nearly five months ago. This is about to become an interesting case, Hunt. Now you had better get on back to Watchampton station; your train is due in twenty minutes time. I'll keep in daily touch with you and we'll also keep on looking for your Jayne Barton."

"Thank you Sir. Every minute that child's life is in danger; the quicker we find her or her body, the better."

# EIGHT

London was bombed again, this time a heavy raid. Inspector Hunt was caught in the centre of it, and was lucky to have survived it with his life. Many people died that evening. He was fortunate to obtain a lift home to Watchampton, even if it was in an empty cattle lorry.

He went straight back to work at the police station which was quiet, especially after London. "You're back then Hunt," the super sounded gritty "You'll find all the messages for you on your desk when you get there, that is."

"Thank you sir. I'm on call twenty four hours a day from now, London said. We are not getting any clues as to the missing child's whereabouts, but as you have heard we found her stepmother's body in the cellar of her own flat. The Met are continuing to help us with the search for Jayne, but the body was on their patch, so they have taken over."

Hunt went through the messages but found nothing new to go on. Most of the sitings were look-alikes and drew blanks but there was piece of information: Hunt had asked for help with a name in the notebook which he had found in Jayne's bedroom. It was the name Brian, and making enquiries around, the detectives at the Met had discovered that Brian was the name of a younger brother of Sid Beech and that he was a taxi driver.

Hunt worked on for another hour, and then told his boss that he must go and tell Iris, as she was Jayne's foster mother. She had to know of the death of Jayne's stepmother. The Super was not in favour, and said it should be kept silent until after the funeral. Jayne's father should be the first to know as the body belonged to him as her next of kin. Hunt did his best to explain about Jayne's father and just how ill he was.

"Then I leave it to you, Hunt."

"Yes Sir. I'll be off now."

Iris was home after her long morning shift at the hospital and she and Rose were just making a cup of tea when DI Hunt called.

"Good news?" They echoed the words together; their face's filled with hope. The two women just stood waiting, while he took over the moment as a policeman. Years on the beat had left him with lack of sentiment. "You had better sit down," he said. "We have some unpleasant news now that I have to tell you."

Rose seemed to crumple; her face went blank as she stared at Hunt while Iris, on the other hand, held herself straight and immediately said, "Let's get on with it: Is Jayne dead? That is the point."

"What I'm about to tell you, has nothing to do with Jayne's position. It concerns her stepmother. We discovered her dead body in the cellar of their flat in Montlake." There was a stunned silence; neither of the women even moved, they just sat staring at Hunt. "Well, my apologies for having to give you this news," he said. Iris was about to reply, but Rose butted in swiftly with an opinion that rocked the room.

"Thanks for telling us the good news! You play with fire, you get burnt. She was a cruel ———."

Iris sprang to her feet. "Now that's enough Granny, don't be rude and let us down, even if we didn't like the woman."

Inspector Hunt raised his eyebrows. "It seems you two ladies know more than I do on this part of the case. However, I like your spirit. At least you speak your mind with gusto as well."

"I only ever speak the truth," muttered Rose.

For the next hour there were a lot of truths told, as they unwrapped all the stories surrounding Jayne's past few years, all the cruelty and injustice that ruled her life.

Later, when Inspector Hunt walked back into the station, the Super kept quiet; he knew by the look on his DI's face, that it was best to keep out of the way. Hunt closed his office door and got straight down to the call from London, as he could see there was fresh information. The message simply said, "Good bit of detective work. That Brian is not what he seems to be on the surface Also, his name's Brian Beech, brother to our suspect Sidney Beech of Montlake. Brian is a taxi driver, but with rather a full wallet."

Hunt placed a sheet of paper in his typewriter and for some reason; he felt good and twenty years younger.

The atmosphere in the house was tight. Rose was sulking and Iris was trying to heal her grandmother's hot head; she was a lovely old lady and Iris hated it when cross words were spoken. It was a moment of fate, when suddenly Ted Hatch tapped on the door and

came in to see them. "No work today?" he asked Iris.

"Yes later Ted, I'm on night duty."

"Gwen sent this," he said, uncovering a large dish covered with pork sausages, homemade. "Farmer gave us these, he made with their own pig." He grinned and winked his eye at Rose. "Poor man ran over one of the young ones with his tractor."

"Poor old farmer, what would the minister of agriculture say?" laughed Rose.

"Send a wreath, of course," said Iris, with a sad straight face. The two women laughed over a cup of tea with their cherished neighbour of many years, while he told them his news. "I've been and bought that car at the garage," he said with a chuckle.

"Good God! How much did that cost you?" asked Iris.

"If my Gwen was here, she would say, 'money and fair words'". "That's a real old saying; now tell us the modern version."

Ted looked at Rose, "Right! Another cup of tea and a slice of that cake you made and I'm all yours."

"How do you know I baked a cake?"

"I could smell its perfume when I opened the back door," he said with a laugh. Iris went out and came back with the tea and three slices of Rose's still warm cake.

"We don't want to know Ted," Iris said. "You're more than welcome, you know."

He pulled a piece of paper out of his pocket. "It was forty nine pounds twelve shillings and sixpence," he said handing the paper to Rose. "Mind you, that was counting the insurance and a drop of petrol. Not bad eh' for a Morris Eight, a nineteen thirty seven car."

"Lot of money," said Rose.

"Yes ladies, but I didn't sell the sow, even if she does shake her head whenever I mention babies. 'Too old,' she moans, at least that is what I think she says when her mouth works overtime.

"It will be nice for Gwen; you can take her out for a spin now and again."

"She already has made plans for that," he gave out a deep sigh. "It's to be a ride up to Frogham every eve to see her sister Gladys, but her sister Glad never did make me glad, she's a measly miserable creature, never liked me. I've started to wish I never bought the thing."

The two women laughed at him. "Typical man," said Rose.

Iris knew that she must visit Jayne's father, especially now while she was still on night duty as it meant that she had days free to travel. She told Rose, knowing what she would say.

"My dear girl what if he asks after his daughter? You know very well, it would kill him to hear his little Jayne had been abducted.

"He's not going to know," Iris said sharply. "Even if I have to tell a white lie."

"You know how I feel about liars," muttered Rose.

Iris got her coat and handbag, and then made for the door. Determined to go, she ran for the bus at the bottom of the road and sat by the window. There weren't many people on the bus but they all knew her. It was what she expected– they were eager to know if she had any news about Jayne. It caused a knot in her stomach and a few tears, which she tried to hide.

When the bus drew into the market place at Watchampton, Iris got off to get on another out of town one. Once again she sat by the window and tried to keep her thoughts on the view as the bus went through lovely countryside. All the time Iris was thinking of Jayne's daddy. Silly really, the child would still call him daddy, nothing would change it, and even though Iris had told her she was now too old for that. Jayne had given her one of her looks and had said, "You think I'm going to say 'my dad', don't you? But I'm not. He is 'Daddy', so there!"

The bus started to slow down and finally stopped near the hospital, a red brick building surrounded by trees and fields. It was so quiet and she walked up the narrow lane with her heart beating fast. The big doors to the hospital were open and a voice behind her said softly, "Can I help you?" It was a tall thin man in a white coat who said, "It's only family visitors I'm afraid."

"I've come to see William Barter," she hesitated and found herself shaking. "I have paid a visit to Mr Barter once before, if you remember. I came with Margaret Jones; her husband was in the next bed."

"Oh yes, and you are?"

"Iris Randall."

"Follow me and I'll see if he's awake."

"How is he?" enquired Iris. There was a brief silence.

"He's making a slow progress."

When she arrived at the bedside, Iris looked down at the man on the bed they called Bob.

"I'll fetch a nurse to stay with you," the doctor said with a smile.

"Hello, we have met before," said Iris. The sound of their voices woke him up.

"You have a visitor Mr Barton." The nurse helped him to sit up. He lifted his thin hand and his face now clear of dressings broke in to a wide smile. "My lucky day," he said, "but do we know each other?"

"I'm Iris Randall, I've been your daughter's foster mother since the bombing, London has had a few bombs," she skirted round that bit not to alarm him. "Now you must hurry up and get well, then you can take over."

He took her hand. "Bring her to see me Iris."

"Yes when I can, but we have to get special permission first. No children allowed in here," she said

"I had forgotten that." He looked deeply into her eyes and she felt a wave of gentle love flow through her body. His limp hand now became more alive. She pulled it away and reached for the bag of fruit she had brought him.

"I remember you now Iris, you brought me fruit once before. I am sorry, but I'm afraid I was not with it then, it is all a bit cloudy. Thank you. I have a lot to thank you for Iris".

"Has the man in the next bed gone home?" she asked. "Mr Jones, wasn't it? I grew to like his wife Margaret." For a moment she wondered if he had heard her, as he made no reply, then suddenly he reached out for her hand again. "Home... .Yes I guess that is what one would call it." His face changed so that he seemed almost a stranger. It alarmed Iris, so she said "Sorry," thinking he was feeling emotional as he remembered a fellow pilot leaving the hospital before him.

"Don't be sad, he was not alone. The war has taken quite a lot of brave men. I shall miss him, old 'bats ears'"

Iris felt as if she had been hit with a brick. "But I thought..."

"Yes we all did, he was so much better, then his heart gave out; it was worse than the meds thought." In the next moment he had put it away from his mind and was back to earth. "You will come and see me every week?"

"I may not be able to do that. I am a hospital nurse; this week it was easy for me. I'm on night duty all this week."

He looked surprised, then rather guilty. "You should be having some sleep instead of coming all this way to visit me. You really are a wonderful girl."

"Flattery will get you nowhere," she joked.

"Once again then, thank you Iris."

She started to move. "I must go now or I shall miss my bus." She let go of his hand and it was then she had another shock.

"Thanks for today," he whispered. "You have helped me during a very emotional time, what with my old mate passing away, and then my wife being found dead, it all came at once like a knife in my side." Iris just couldn't believe it, here she was tying herself up in knots, her hands shaky, all because of her fear about telling Bob of his wife's death and he knew all the time. Inspector Hunt must have been to see him. She grabbed the hard back of the chair to

89

steady herself. "That is what I came to tell you," she stuttered, "and you knew. I've been through hell trying to pluck up courage to give you the news, such sad news too."

"Well, I'm so glad you were here, as it is one of those deaths where the emphasis is not on grief, but a pain inside the body. You see, it was never a good marriage, more of a bad mistake. Please sit down and hear me out Iris."

"I'll miss my bus," she said.

"Never mind, I can order you a taxi from here."

Iris sat on the edge of the chair, but listened to his story. "I came home on a forty hour leave just to see how Jayne was, and found her locked in the cupboard. My so-called wife had also hit her; Jayne had bruises on her face and arms. We had a terrible row and the dentist from up in the flat above came down to find out the reason for all the noise. He's a very nice man, has always been friendly, and loves Jayne. To cut the story short, he agreed to visit my flat every day and night, so as to make sure that Jayne was all right. Clare never hurt my child again, but we were finished. I contacted the child welfare and they said it was all exaggerated and that Jayne was quite happy."

Iris could bear no more, the irony of it all, and how the hand of fate just used the situation for a deeper evil, just felt like a clip round the face. With a swift movement she started to leave. "Goodbye, I will come again." She gathered her things and fled. If she ran she would just make it to the bus stop. Fortunately, the driver saw her coming and waited for her.

.

The warmth of the house, and the gorgeous smell of cooking, were all Iris needed as she pulled off her coat and looked for her grandmother.

"Oh Gran!" Iris flung her arms around her, nearly knocking her backwards. When she called her 'Gran', then Rose knew that there was grief or despair.

"What's up my dear girl?"

"I've had such a day, too much emotion and surprise."

"How is Jayne's daddy?"

"He's certainly improving, but my God gran, there is so much he still doesn't know in his life. However, there's no time now to tell you the whole story, as you know I have to go to work tonight, and that's in less than an hour."

"Have you had any food all day?"

"No. I must, though really I don't feel like it."

"I do have a lovely meal for you, so you must try dear." Rose looked concerned as she coaxed her to eat the plate of hot fried fish. "Do you know who gave us that?" she said to Iris. "It was Ted; he has been to fish market today."

"Yes of course, in his new car," grinned Iris. "It's only four pence on the bus. It will take him years to get his forty odd pounds back, Granny."

The thought of going to work all night, lay heavily on her shoulders. She knew what the conversation would be among the nurses; it would start with, "Have they had any news of Jayne? Any sightings?" Iris knew she had to put a brave face on it, but the hurt and memories would not go away. Just for a brief moment she thought of the thin pale figure of Bob sitting up in bed; she still felt the slim fingers winding round her own hand. It left a strange feeling inside and she realised that her heart was beating faster. She felt sure that the nurse beside her could see it thumping under her blouse.

It was a fortnight since Iris had paid that emotional visit to William. She felt guilty at not keeping her promise to visit. It was made more difficult by the change in her work time table; she was now on duty nearly all day. The hospital had extra patients who had been admitted, due to the casualties from the air raid in the adjoining village.

On hearing the drop of the letter box she went to see what mail they had. Iris picked up the one letter and went back to the kitchen. "Is that for me?" asked Rose.

" No. It's addressed to me." They both fingered it, studied it, looked at the postmark and eventually Rose said, "For heaven's sake girl! Open it."

Surprised, she read the tender little letter from Bob. He had worried in case he had driven her away with his talk about Clare. He was suffering guilt and begged her to come and see him, this time bringing Jayne.

"Oh Gran, what can I do?" It's all too complicated. It will also mean telling him all the drama and worry surrounding Jayne. Not easy." With a cry of sheer despair, she handed the letter to Rose to read. "Why oh why can't they find Jayne?"

Rose set her lips in a thin line, her anger showing in her face. "I'm going across the field to Ted," she said. "He's got a telephone; I shall ring the station and give them a piece of my mind. That Inspector Hunt is not pushing it enough, it's time he let the newspaper know."

"Hang on Granny, Jayne is more likely to be in London and Inspector Hunt has been co-operating with the London police for a long time and even been up there."

But there was no stopping Rose when she made up her mind. The next thing was the sound of the back door closing with a bang.

# NINE

D.I. Hunt returned to London; there were quite a few letters from the general public offering their help or informing them that they had seen Sidney Beech. Of course they had proved to be look-alikes, so the waste bin became full. There was one letter that did interest Hunt: It was from someone who said he knew someone who fitted the police description of Beech and that this man regularly changed his appearance by wearing different glasses and sometimes had a beard or moustache. It turned out to be another person very much like Sid but it had given Hunt an idea. He turned the word 'disguise' round in his head. This was a good bit of news. Now he was at least prepared.

There was a knock on the office door. It was a constable with the news that he had just seen someone go into Sid's flat; he and the rest of the force had been told to keep a keen eye on the house made into two flats.

Hunt moved swiftly gathering help on the way. He took three plain-clothes policemen with him and they sped up the road, where they found a perfect parking spot in between two old vans, one of which was unloading a tray of large two-gallon loaves of fresh bread in to a baker's shop. It was a busy road but Hunt never took his eyes off the big green double doors of the flats.

They had been there over an hour with no sign of movement from the flats when suddenly it happened: A man in dark navy blue overalls came out of big doors wearing a flat cap with long white hair creeping from under it; he was also holding a workman's tool-bag and a small length of pipe.

"That's not him," said one of the officers in the van. Hunt shot his hand out and grabbed the door; he was cool but the look in his eyes spelt fire. "Now listen," he said sharply, "it's someone in disguise and I'm convinced it's Sidney Beech. I'm going in first and you can support me by mixing with the crowd not less than ten feet away from me. I think he's going to get in one of those cars or that van. Go!"

The crowd gave him cover as he walked casually among them. Sid was walking with head down and making for a small Morris Eight that was parked near the curb just in front of Hunt, then he hung back just long enough for Sid to find the key in his pocket and as he put it in the door of the car, he placed a hand on his arm. "I'd like you to come with me to the station for questioning sir." Beech was taken by surprise; his self confidence shattered in a second and he could see the two policemen in plain clothes, now standing by the car.

Hunt cuffed him for safety sake and they took him back to the station in the police van. "You can take that cap off now, and the wig," said Hunt.

"Damn you," muttered Beech. "How did you know it was me?"

" That nose!" said Hunt, "it reveals the feature of a one-time boxer, which you were." After the cuffs were put on, the two officers bundled him in their van and took him back to the station for questioning, where he was body-searched and found to have one broken half of a necklace in his coat pocket, evidence of his part in the murder of Clare Barton, Jayne's stepmother. "So that's what you went back to the flat for! You knew it was evidence that would help convict you." Hunt looked at him in disgust. "Now we want to know what you have done with Jayne and I am not leaving until I get some answers!" He banged the table with his clenched fist, making Beech jump. "What have you done with Jayne?"

Later that afternoon, Hunt prepared to leave the station; there was no more he could do at the moment. Beech had been charged with the murder of Clare Barton. Hunt was hungry, he hadn't rested or eaten all day; the little homely boarding house he had got used to in London was cheap and the food was plain but good. As he got up and reached for his coat, about to leave the room, the Super called him into his office. It made Hunt wonder whatever he was going to say, as there was an unusual grin on the Super's naturally dour face.

"What do you think, Hunt? I've just been reading the coroner's final report. I must say I had a surprise: Well, previously I had only looked at it quickly, but there is no doubt in my mind, Beech strangled Clare Barton and broke the necklace in the process. The imprints on the dead woman's neck match up with that necklace that you found in Jayne's trinket box. There was one little indent with another in the circle mark, identifiable with the necklace. He must have put an enormous pressure on her throat and that was what snapped the chain. The coroner says that two tiny pieces of metal, maybe gold plated were taken from her throat. We've got him this time! Beech is covering for his brother Brian. He insists that he doesn't know where his brother lives now as he had been bombed out twice and had to find another house."

Hunt could hardly argue on this factor. All he could do was wait while investigations continued.

" Well I really must ring my wife Sir, she will be worried as London is rather a dangerous place to be it seems." He thought about his young eight year old daughter; he missed her, his shadow, she always seemed to follow him wherever he went in the house, even appearing with his slippers. The trouble was, he was rarely at home and when he was, he was forever getting called out. He pushed away the feeling of tiredness. It was nice to be needed.

# TEN

Jayne always came down for breakfast as soon as Brian banged on her door at seven; then she would hear him turn the key to let her out. Bread to make toast was the menu from day to day, rarely any butter left so she smothered it with jam. Brian generally had his breakfast at the cafe just down the road. He looked so different in the mornings with his bald head and shabby suit which made him look a stranger, Jayne kept her distance from him, but he was soon away, until two pm.

She pulled herself up from the table and stared out of the kitchen window. Sunshine was creeping in and reflecting off something on the floor which caught her eye. It was a ring with two keys and she picked them up, wondering which locks they fitted. With her heart beating fast, she tried the windows then the back door and others, until she suddenly realized that the larger one was the spare key to the front door which he must have dropped the night before! He never left any keys lying about for her to escape and Jayne started shaking with both fear and excitement as she held her freedom in the palm of her hand. She noticed that her hands were shaking. She ran up the passage and tried it in the front door. It did fit! She opened the door but locked it again, deciding the need to go back for a warm coat was essential, besides, he could come back without warning. Grabbing the coat from the hook on the kitchen door, she was starting to panic.

Moving towards the door again, she heard a key click in the lock from outside. He was at the door! Quickly she put the coat back and the keys on the dresser. She decided to play it cool and calm and not let him think she was scared of him.

"Keys," he yelled out as he came into the room, towering over her, red with anger. "Have you found any keys lying around?"

Jayne was eating the cold toast and had her mouthful, so she nodded her head. He was so angry. "Come on child, answer me. Where are they then?"

"I found them on the floor so I put them on the dresser. What are they for?"

He glared at her. "One is the key to my desk at my office which I needed this morning and the larger one is the front door key. I have two."

"Perhaps they fell out of your trouser pocket last night, as you do hang them on that chair near the fire."

"How do you know that?" His hand was raised above Jayne so that she thought for a minute he was going to hit her.

"I came down one night for a drink of water, so I noticed them, and NO I didn't look in the pockets, I don't do that sort of thing."

Grabbing the keys he went out, but on his way he looked at the butter on the table, telling her to go easy on it as it was his rations she was eating.

For the next few days it remained dry and sunny: The weather had certainly changed in Jayne's favour, as the sun shone into the kitchen each day giving inspiration to her plans to escape; even the strips of sticky paper across the glass which were there to help prevent the glass from flying out if the house was bombed, made no difference to the sun as it turned into beams of light.

Jayne sat thinking just how she could open the window, even if it meant picking the lock on it. What she needed was some tools but she didn't know where to find any. Then she recalled the day when her father took two tools from her late mother's sewing machine; there was a little compartment inside filled with them. She remembered how her mother had told him to leave her sewing machine alone and he was in the dog house for the whole day. The memory made Jayne laugh. She searched every cupboard in the house and luck was with her as she found a small screwdriver in a drawer, which she hurriedly slipped into the pocket of her skirt. She had a dreadful task ahead and was now really scared, because if he came back , he would kill her.

No one could ever call her a coward, and with a deep breath she grabbed a small chair, stood on it and made a shaky start with the screwdriver on the oblong shape that was locked. Listening all the time for that key in the front door, her efforts were rewarded as it moved a tiny bit. Once or twice she nearly gave up; she felt sick, her shoulder was aching, her fingers were sore. Then it clicked and she had accomplished an enormous task with no other knowledge than watching her father open their store-cupboard one day; she had remembered all the details and was glad she had.

The next task was to raise the lower half of this sash window. However, it was not as easy as it looked! It hadn't been opened for a long time, so she pulled and pulled. Once again she stopped to think then dashing in to the larder, she buttered a short blunt knife with the intention of prizing the window upwards. It worked! But now was the most dangerous moment. If he came home now. . . . she was helpless and finished.

It worked. Slowly the frame came up and there was a flush of fresh air, but there was no time to stand and stare, she must be off away fast. She grabbed her coat from the back of the kitchen door and was out of the window in seconds.

The feeling of freedom and fresh air was heavenly but now she felt more scared than ever. Running round to the back garden she discovered that she could get out along the side of the house right on to the road. Now for a real escape. The thing was, she must turn left because he always turned right when he left in the mornings; the last thing she needed was to bump into him.

The sun poured its warmth and approval on to Jayne as she walked quickly up the long road; there was no need to run as she would only draw attention to herself. The road began to widen and she could see double-decker buses running in the cross roads ahead, which made her think : The best thing would be to jump on a bus and go as far away from the area as possible. Feeling in her coat pocket she was relieved to find some small change. Her idea was to get off the moment she spotted a police station. Now there was joy in her heart at the thought of contacting the policeman, DI Hunt, who she liked and who was no doubt searching the country for her.

The bus conductress charged her four pence for her ticket. Jayne couldn't tell her where she wanted to get off but she was told to ring the bell. It was quite a long ride and her eyes had been scouring the scenery, when suddenly she saw it between two large blocks of offices. A police station! The bus stopped for her and she found herself in a busy shopping area with only a short distance to walk there. She stood a few yards away from the entrance, where three policemen were trying to control a very large man and though he was handcuffed he was being difficult so Jayne stood well away from the" crowd that was gathering. It was no good even thinking of entering the small police station at that moment so she decided that she would have to wait around for the right time. She was lucky because no one seemed to recognize her. She had wondered if her photo was in the newspapers so, keeping her head down, Jayne was soon lost in the crowd. At that moment a woman behind her touched her shoulder, making her turn round. "Are you lost?" asked the elderly lady, her eyes stark and staring as she looked Jayne up and down. A moment later and she had hold of her tightly and was trying to pull Jayne away. "Come with me and I'll take you home girlie. Got any money?"

Jayne tried to get away. The passers-by didn't help. One just muttered, "Grandchildren! A right handful sometimes."

Jayne changed her play, deciding to smooth talk this strange woman, so she said, "I'll give you some of my money, but you'll have to let go of me as it is in my petticoat pocket. I have to get to it." With a little play-acting Jayne lifted her skirt and moved her hand to the petticoat. . . then she ran, taking the woman by surprise and, making for a large store, she dashed inside. But her unwanted friend was behind her! And could she run for an elderly lady.

Inside this department store there were plenty of places to hide; one of them was a big display of grey blankets so she crawled in the back of the pile. The woman thought Jayne had gone in the moving lift, so off she went, causing a disturbance among the few customers. Two of the staff were having a conversation nearby and Jayne listened as she remained hidden. Apparently the woman was no stranger to the store and was considered to be unstable, due to the loss of her little grandchild in an air raid, during which a bomb had taken the rest of her family.

Jayne showed herself and spoke to one of the staff about the situation. They took her to the manager in his office where she could unfold the rest of her story.

"Then you are the missing girl who was kidnapped a couple of months ago?" said the manager. He phoned the police and two officers with a plain-clothed man in charge came to take Jayne to safety.

The woman had been caught but she looked a sad mess, the hairpins in her hair had fallen out and her grey, unclean hair was hanging round her neck. Jayne felt a pain of sadness run through her and she called out to the officers not to charge the woman as she not hurt her, but they just smiled and remained silent.

Once back at the police station Jayne was made a lot of fuss of, but she was so tired and suffering from lack of food that she shut her eyes several times. A Red Cross lady brought her a bowl of hot soup and some bread which she thanked her for. It was some time before DI Hunt arrived from Watchampton but when he did he was so pleased to see the little girl he had admired and liked from the first day he saw her.

When he arrived, she was sitting there among the officers, showing them how to pick a lock on a window with a screwdriver!

It was a terrible journey back to Watchampton. It meant going through bombed areas and sometimes detouring around an impassable bombed road. Jayne could not understand, but there had been quite a lot of destruction in parts that had not been touched before. It suddenly struck her just how many months she had been held prisoner. A lot had happened during that time. She talked to Hunt when the roads were quiet and she told him how frightened she had been of Sid's brother who had lured her away from the market that fateful day.

The thought of seeing her father had made her jump straight in the car. They discussed her father and she pleaded with him to take her to see him, but he tried to explain just how ill he was.

"Let's just get you home first. Granny Rose is longing to see you, she has been through a very bad time of worry and grief. A lovely lady," said Hunt. "I've known her quite a few years. She's so looking forward to seeing you. Actually she didn't think she would ever again; we've had tears and questions as to why I had not found you."

They were approaching a very busy area, so Jayne sat back in her seat and remained quiet for a while, but once they got into the country outskirts Hunt started conversation again.

"Did you see your step-mother that evening before Uncle Sid took you to Watchampton? You said she was asleep in her chair."

"I couldn't get near her you see, as uncle Sid stood in front of her and kept me away from her; he also told me that we must leave her quiet as she had not been very well." There was a pause for a moment, then Jayne said in a slightly embarrassed tone, "There wasn't much wrong with her a half hour before; she was laughing and letting Sid jump about on her in her bedroom. The door was wide open. My real mother always closed it when her and my father went in their bedroom."

There was a smile on the detective's face. It was quiet for a few minutes, then Jayne said sharply, "He thought he was so clever but he didn't see me pick up one of the broken pieces of necklace from the floor beside her. The other piece was under the wardrobe where I couldn't reach it without bending down. Then he would have seen me pick it up. It was my real mother's and father gave it to her not long before she died. I think she took it from my mother's trinket box that was still on the dressing table. I wish I knew where the other half went."

Hunt made no reply, but his thoughts were stirred.

The journey was a long one, as Hunt knew it would be; the trains were insecure, bombed lines and stations were open targets for the enemy planes. By now it was quite dark; there were only the stars above to give light since the wartime rules forbade any street lighting at all; if you needed to be out after dark, you took a small torch and only shone it on the ground.

He told Jayne to be quiet for a while as he had to concentrate and before long, when he looked across at her again, she was asleep.

Back at last in Watchampton, the next hour was spent at the police station, taking statements from Jayne and waiting for Iris to arrive to take Jayne back home. A woman P.C. who had been assigned to look after the child asked her why she had been kidnapped and whether she knew if Brian had demanded money for her return.

Of course, Jayne didn't know but she did raise a few eyebrows when she told all of her story: With a sigh, she told them that she thought her kidnap was a business deal between Brian and his brother Sid, to make money out of her healing hands. There was a silence, broken only at last by Jayne's explanation.

"They made me wear a wig so that people wouldn't recognise me then I had to go with Brian to strange houses and perform a healing touch on sick or injured people. They were nearly all old people but he took the money from them all the same and it was a lot of money too. You see, I can heal people; it does work most of the time except for very old people and then it's not my fault."

The look on the faces of the officers in the interview room said it all: This child had been through so much and yet was still so young, despite her adult outlook on life. She was clearly highly intelligent and understood the implications of her story, as it affected the two brothers.

By this time there was a little gathering outside the station, as people had heard the news and were pleased the little girl Jayne had been found. In the meantime there were still a lot of questions to be asked; although Jayne had been found, there was still the matter of bringing the criminals to justice and a doctor had been called to make sure that Jayne was fit and well enough to go home. Jayne shed tears, but somehow was not sure why; all that mattered was her sudden longing to see Iris again and to hold her beloved daddy.

# ELEVEN

Jayne's homecoming was a special day, one that she would remember for the rest of her life. Whilst it was a happy day, there was an undercurrent of sadness, which lingered in the room as if waiting to burst like a cloud of cold rain.

The room was full of neighbours and friends who had gathered to welcome Jayne home, but they noticed the look of pain on the faces of Iris and Rose. The two women were on edge waiting for Jayne to ask for her daddy and of course it was one of the first things she did.

"Why didn't Daddy come and see me?"

Rose broke the silence by going across and taking her hand. "He would have been here, only he is in hospital, dear. He is a bit poorly."

"Why didn't you tell me? You must have known I need to see him," Jayne snapped. Shock had turned to anger and turning away from the granny she loved and pushing her in a temper, she ran out of the room and up the stairs to her bedroom.

Iris followed her and tried to comfort her by assuring her that they were going to see daddy the next day. "You will be able to talk to him on your own, while I sit and watch."

The gentle words took root, Jayne smiled at Iris, feeling more relaxed. "Are we going on the bus?" she asked.

"No. Mr Hatch is taking us in his new car."

"I'm glad you didn't say, Uncle Ted, because I don't want any more uncles, I've had enough of them, no more uncles, thank you." Iris had to smile. What a strange child she was.

Down in the kitchen Rose had made a large pot of tea while she tried to explain the situation. People all knew her from many years, so they understood. Jayne had suffered so much; her nerves were strained to the limit. Iris came down and admitted that Jayne was asleep already. She had coaxed her to get into bed and rest, so that she would be ready to meet her daddy the next day.

One by one the friendly crowd of people left, leaving Iris and Rose in the kitchen with Ted. "Why did that man Sid bring Jayne to Watchampton in the first place?" Rose asked him.

"That's what I wondered," he replied. "I asked that inspector Hunt and he reckons Sid needed to get her away from the house 'cause he had to dispose of her stepmother's body and the ideal place to hide Jayne was his cottage here in the town. The bloke he had rented it to had left so it was empty. She must have been so scared of that Sid. Course, she knew he was having an affair with her stepmother. Jayne told the police that she was often left alone in the house when Sid and Clare went off partying in London."

Ted has asked if he could see Jayne's father, seeing that he was the one who helped her from the rubble of the bombed house but Iris was careful not to commit herself as they had not had very good news of the patient, who was said to be still on the danger list. Her heart was thumping as she thought of all the risk, taking Jayne to the hospital. What if her father lost his grip on life while they were there?

Rose interrupted her thoughts. "Is Jayne really safe now, or do we have to worry about her safety?"

"Push all those thoughts away," said Iris. "Sidney Beech is about to serve a long sentence for his part in the murder of Jayne's stepmother Clare, and when they catch his brother Brian, he will be on trial for his part in kidnapping and holding Jayne prisoner. He never hurt Jayne and I suppose he fed her well enough but he was exploiting her by earning money from her healing ability; people were paying a lot for a session of her touch. The inspector told me that Sid Beech had left fingerprints on the necklace, which, the police say must have broken in half when he strangled her. Don't forget, Jayne picked up the other piece of necklace on the floor when Sid wasn't looking. She must have thought her stepmother was asleep."

"Will Jayne have to go to court as witness do you think? asked Rose with a shudder.

"No. I had a talk to Inspector Hunt on that subject, and he said that because of her age, she's too young to take the witness stand or appear in court. Of course, she didn't actually witness the murder; Jayne says she thought Clare was asleep in the high-backed chair. The less we talk about it in front of her, the better."

"Poor little child," said Rose. "What a disaster for a young child, who should be out with her school friends playing and chasing the boys. She ought to be told about Sid's arrest and the long prison sentence he'll serve."

"It's her father's place to talk to her about that but of course, she knows a lot more than we think. Never mind," said Iris wiping the tears from her face, "we'll try to make her happy and forget it all. That is if her beloved daddy lives. Perhaps she'll lay her little hands on him to heal his sick body. We'll know tomorrow."

The journey to the hospital was not without problems: Ted had trouble starting the engine up with the heavy metal starting handle. Of course, it had to be raining and resulted in a damp coat and wet hair. This caused a delay, but as Iris explained to Jayne, he had never possessed a car before and had learned to drive himself with his friend at the garage loaning him an old van for a week.

When they eventually arrived at the hospital Iris made inquiries first, concerning Jayne's daddy. Apparently he was still very ill but was a little more stable than the previous day, which was something. Iris asked if his little daughter could see him but the doctor shook his head and frowned.

"He is unable to hold a conversation," he said.

"Please. I promise she will be in control, gentle and understanding," Iris pleaded. The doctor stood tall in front of Iris and was touched by what he saw, mother and child. Or was she?

"You are his wife?" he asked.

"No but I'm Jayne's foster mother," replied Iris. "We are her only next of kin now; you see, her birth mother died two years ago. I am hoping to adopt her if she is left an orphan. I pray her daddy will soon get well."

"Very well, but you must be quiet and not disturb him. I will take you to him." He noticed Jayne was talking to a nurse; he was impressed with her attitude and called her to go with them to the little room next to the main ward.

To give the child her due, she was silent and dignified as they approached the man in the bed. Her cry of, "Daddy!" was so soft, but it held such love and devotion that even the young doctor felt the emotional stab as he stood by the bed. After taking his temperature he pulled up two chairs for them then left the two.

Very soon Jayne began to get restless. She stared hard at her daddy's face, as he seemed such a stranger to her, looking so different. With a swift but silent gesture she leaned across the bed and touched his face, her slim fingers slowly resting on his head. Iris made no move to stop her, but watched in stunned silence as Jayne now gently moved the bedcovers back and placed her hand on his chest, across his heart. This was all done in complete silence, with her hand remaining flat on his body. "My daddy." It was only a whisper, but close to his ear.

The next minute there was a flickering of his eyelids and then he opened both eyes. Jayne was still bending over him and as her eyes met his, he smiled.

"I love you daddy." It was only a whisper, but he heard her. The next moment he changed, relaxed and closed his eyes. Sleep now overtook him, but he had changed, gone was the tightness around his mouth, his lips were softer and the smile was not completely gone.

Iris felt strange, as if her body was not really there in the chair. She moved slightly and put her hand out to make contact with Jayne as they both moved away from the bed. Looking down the corridor Iris could see Ted, who was talking to the young doctor and, as they approached, the doctor apologised for omitting to allow Ted to enter the ward, explaining that only family could be admitted and only two at a time. Ted didn't seem to mind and suggested they soon got back on the road.

Iris spoke about a further visit in a day or two. "We'll go now. I think he will make it, doctor. I hope to see you soon."

Jayne put her hand out to shake the doctor's. "Thank you for letting me stay and see my daddy."

"Well, you see we don't allow children in the hospital. However, you behaved so well that we'll let you come to see your father again in the future, without query."

Jayne was very quiet on the way home, so was Ted. He was disappointed at not being allowed to see Jayne's father as he had a very high respect for the young airmen who risked their lives every day for their country and he was also anxious to meet this beloved 'Daddy.'

It took them longer to get home than by bus, but Ted was afraid of speeding, so drove them slowly home. Iris preferred the bus, but kept her thoughts from overflowing: It was kind of Ted to take them.

Rose was waiting nervously for them and her first words were not exactly "Was he still alive?"

"Of course," said Iris quickly, "and what is more, he is going to get better." Jayne had not heard this banter of conversation; she was in Rose's armchair already sound asleep. When Iris carried her upstairs to her bed, she was rather surprised at the child's loss of weight; she was very thin, the result of her abduction as they had certainly not fed her properly.

A sudden thought struck Iris: Jayne had given out a lot of healing power and also her strength in the process. As Iris tucked her up, it made her determined to give her extra care as she needed feeding up.

In the morning, she made up her mind to call the doctor and let him examine Jayne. It was a wise decision in calling out their local doctor, just to give Jayne a medical examination. Iris was feeling the responsibility as she was, after all, only Jayne's foster parent and her health and well being was essential.

The doctor recommended that Jayne needed extra care, good food and cod liver oil, plus vitamin C found in orange juice. These would be provided at the local welfare office, free of charge.

Jayne soon picked up her body weight again and with Rose's good cooking she soon looked a great deal stronger.

Rose remarked one morning that Jayne was more like her old self, as she kept on talking about her beloved daddy.

"I need to go and see him," she told Iris.

What Rose and Jayne did not know, was that Iris had been keeping in contact with the hospital to find out if William Barton was recovering, even if she had her doubts to start with. He was, rapidly. The doctors and staff considered it to be a miracle. Not only was he out of bed, but gaining strength every day. It was the talk of the whole hospital. There was a feeling of excitement but an important question was in everyone's thoughts: Was this the result of Jayne's healing hands?

Iris decided the time had come for Jayne to visit her daddy. Rose told Ted Hatch, so he offered to take them and Iris was pleased, because she felt it was time he was introduced to Jayne's daddy, after all he had been involved in her rescue.

They decided to make the journey over on the following Sunday, as it was the whole day off for Iris, also the hospital was not so full at the time. It was a nice journey, with the spring sunlight shining on the fresh growing leaves, making the scenery around them fresh and green.

When they arrived at the large red brick house, Ted made a remark on the unconventional place for a service hospital. Iris agreed, but went on to explain to Ted the reason for it being tucked down in the centre of a belt of trees, quiet and off the beaten track. "Some of the patients have been on secret missions," she told him, "so they have to be nursed, away from the public eye. You are not allowed to take photos here or in the vicinity," said Iris. "That was why they didn't allow you in before, Ted."

When they approached the big oak door to the building, the same doorman let them in, after taking their names and the full name of the patient they were there to visit. He hesitated over Ted Hatch, but let him in when the head of medical staff came and welcomed them inside, including Ted.

As they walked into the large entrance hall, Iris was amazed at the murmur of voices and the group of patients and staff who had apparently gathered to welcome Jayne, all staring at them. She ran towards them all, excited and looking for her daddy. They held out their hands to touch her, calling out her name. "Jayne, Jayne."

One of the men in a wheelchair pointed to the small armchair behind them. "There's your daddy," he said.

Jayne ran to him and smothered him with kisses. Iris waited a few minutes before going to him; she was eager to introduce him to Ted as he had played a large part in Jayne's life after the air raid.

At last, Iris was alone with the man she had grown to love; he was so like his amazing daughter, who was now talking to the patients in a tone way above her years. She was discussing the effect of a sick body and the power of the mind. One of the pilots was heard to say, "How old is that child? Seven years of age! I don't believe it."

The hall cleared as the men went back to their own rooms. Jayne was having another discussion with a doctor, who agreed to allow her daddy home that day. Ted had just finished a long conversation with one of the patients and with Jayne's daddy. Ted had offered to come any time and bring him back to meet Rose and to see Iris.

Back in his own room, William had a chance to talk alone with Iris. "You do know," he said softly, "I have fallen in love with you Iris. I only hope you feel the same way."

"Yes," she whispered as she brushed her lips across his. "I fell for you from the minute I first saw you."

"Will you marry me?" he said, stumbling on the words with emotion.

"Yes of course, when you are finished with hospitals."

He took her in his arms as he said, "Ready made family, I'm afraid. Do you mind?"

"No, that is the best bit. I love your daughter to bits. Jayne has already become part of my life. I would not part with her for all the money in the world."

"Looks like I've got competition," he said before his lips met hers.

As they left the hospital, Jayne said goodbye to the doctors and nurses.

"That is my mummy and daddy," Jayne told them all with pride as she left her newly found friends to join Iris.

The journey home in Ted's little car was unusually quiet; Jayne had drawn heavily on her emotions and it had taken her strength, so she had closed her eyes but still clutched her father's hand. William understood and had nothing but admiration for his brave little daughter.

Iris sat in the front of the car next to Ted as he was unsure of the road and she helped to guide him through the twisting lanes and turnings.

They arrived at the cottage which was going to be home for William for the next three weeks. He intended to go back to his squadron as soon as he could and was intent on getting to grips with the enemy. He retained his willpower in spite of his frailty at the moment.

Iris expected to see her grandmother standing on the doorstep waiting for them. It was the sort of thing that she did; but she was not there. They found her asleep in her armchair. Rose got up full of apologies and after being introduced to William, she went out of her way to make him comfortable in her armchair with lots of cushions. Ted could not stay; he disliked leaving his car outside, afraid that someone would take it, but he did promise Iris that he would come back after tea, bringing his wife Gwen, who was eager to meet William.

Jayne was still clinging to her father even while asleep on the couch. When she woke up Iris pulled her away and as a diversion she took her upstairs to see where her father would be sleeping. It was quite an emotional moment for Iris. Jayne suddenly asked her if she could sleep in there with him, but Iris, taken off guard for a second, said rather sharply that she couldn't. They went in to the next bedroom which was Iris's and she rummaged in her little trinket box to find a pretty little child's bracelet, which was gold and very suitable for Jayne, so she gave it to her, asking her to promise that she would look after it.

"Oh thank you mummy I shall treasure it". Iris stood speechless for a moment, she had called her 'mummy'. Never had Jayne said that before, it took her breath away a bit.

They went back downstairs to the kitchen just in time for the meal which Rose was dishing up, scrambled eggs, one each. William stared at the food before saying, "Eggs, my goodness, they are rationed too, we only had one egg a week and that was what was known as dried eggs." Iris enjoyed telling him that there were fifteen chickens out in the field laying eggs. He would be able to give a hand looking after them when he was stronger. There was happy laughter at the table, very relaxing thought William.

Time went so quickly. Ted and Gwen came as promised and she was introduced to Iris's fiance. She noted how smart he was in his full uniform of the Royal Air Force. He was quite a good looking young man too, even with the long red scar running down the side of his face. It was still very raw, time would be needed for it to heal completely.

Gwen noticed how he talked to everyone without turning his face and she wondered if that was the reason that Rose had sat on his injured side.

During the evening Rose cleared the table as she had some documents to go through with them. Ted and Gwen got up from the table to leave, saying that it was time that they went. However, Rose insisted they stay as of course they were old friends and they would find it interesting.

Rose pulled the thick paper out on to the table, and then informed Iris that she was going to sign over her cottage to Iris now instead of leaving it to her in her will. "We shall go on as usual and I will still live here for my last few years but," she said, "you will always have a roof over your head, well, for you and William. I take it that you will not be going back to London?" William looked relieved and made it clear that he could never enter that London house ever again, adding how kind Rose was to them. The future did not look so bleak, not forgetting however, the war was not over yet.

Ted and Gwen now made moves to go home and after a few affectionate hugs and goodnights they made their way out. Jayne was still up; they had left her sleeping and before he left, Ted carried her upstairs to her little bed. Iris had left a tiny night light by her bedsi.de, knowing her fear of the dark.

Iris walked out of the back door with Ted and Gwen. It was a beautiful night, the full moon picked out the dark shape of the trees and the rooftops. There were thousands of stars.

"Hope we don't get Jerry over here tonight. It is just right for them," said Ted.

Gwen put her arm round Iris as she stood there looking across the field at Ted's cottage. It was a soft voice, almost a whisper when she spoke to Iris. "My help and my loving friendship will always be there for you Iris. You know you have taken on a big task. Don't forget I am not far away." Iris stood there until they had walked across the little field and were in their cottage. The glow of their oil lamp shone through the thin curtains. Iris turned and opened the back door. There was a tear running down her cheek, which she wiped quickly away. There was no time for tears, she had a family now to look after and there was her Jayne, the little girl she had always wanted and had waited for so long.

## THE END